SHATTERED

Donna Augustine

This book is a work of fiction. All names, characters, places, and incidents are products of the author's imagination and used fictitiously. Any resemblance to actual events, people or places is entirely coincidental.

ISBN: 0615921450
ISBN-13: 978-0615921457
Strong Hold Publishing

For my mother, who swears I'm the most brilliant writer even though she's never read any of my books.

CONTENTS

EDITING BY EXPRESS EDITING

LINE/CONTENT EDITING BY
DEVILINTHEDETAILSEDITING.COM

CHAPTER ONE

I leaned my head back against the leather conference chair as I rested the soles of my boots on the dark mahogany table. The room was packed to bursting, between the leadership of wolves, the Fae and humans. Eyes closed, I tried to listen through the din for specific voices but it was too chaotic to follow. They were all speaking at once.

"Enough," Cormac said, or more accurately, yelled. He very seldom raised his voice but after the week we'd just had, I wasn't surprised he was more on edge than normal.

One week ago today, we had closed the final tear in the universe, located exactly where New York City used to be. The hell that we unleashed was beyond any of our imaginations. Slow death by radiation was looking more and more like it might have been the better choice. That was no longer an option. We'd merged our existence with the plane of magic, and for better or worse, this was the new world, perhaps the *only* world.

There was no way of telling what happened to Vitor's planet. It was too risky to try and open a wormhole now, if it were even possible. What once might have had a predictable outcome was now a game of Russian Roulette. That's what happens when the machine gets all gunked up with extra crap in the engine. In this case, the extra crap happened to be magic.

Magic. Does anyone really even know what it is? If I'd been asked for a definition a year ago, I would have said it was beautiful and impossible things, unicorns frolicking under rainbows and pots of gold guarded by strange little men wearing green. It might still be all of those things...but it was also so much more. It was the ghastly images from nightmares and your deepest fears come to life. And now, it was just your run of the mill day, sitting at a meeting with creatures you didn't know existed a year ago.

The packed conference room fell silent and I forced my heavy eyelids open. Cormac stood, leaning over the table, palms flat on its surface with his head bent down. His shirtsleeves were rolled up as usual, showing off the tense muscular forearms that accented even further how on edge he was, if you hadn't already picked up on his “rip your head off” tone.

If he had been a mentally weaker man, this would've been his breaking point. I know if I thought it was an option, it would've been mine. I've never considered myself a slouch in the stamina department, but my limits were being tested daily.

I looked around the room as the silence continued. This was one of the many "open" meetings we'd had since our return. Everyone would all come in and wait for Cormac to utter some words of brilliance that would make things okay, would make sense of the chaos that ensued after New York. They just didn't get it. There was nothing that was going to make this okay. We'd destroyed something that night and there was no fixing it. This was it.

Burrom, Vitor, Rogo and all their people...the ones still alive that is, had been waiting for us at The Lacard when we finally managed to get back. "We" is what's left of The Keepers, a number that was less than it had been a week ago. We'd lost three just on the way home, not to mention the heap of metal that had once been a shiny 747.

"I don't have any answers," Cormac's voice broke the silence and brought me roughly back to the present.

"What are those grey creatures hovering out there? The ones everyone calls the rippers?" A human named Sally asked. "They *ate* one of my friends! Tore him apart, limb by limb, in front of us."

"I told you, I don't know. We're working on it." Cormac ran a hand through his black hair, the shadow along his jaw darker than normal.

I felt human eyes upon me but ignored them. I had the Fae and wolves' attention as well, and I ignored them too, staring up at the ceiling instead. They all wanted to come here to Earth. So much so, they'd been willing to do it by any means possible. Now that it had turned ugly, they wanted to blame The Keepers for it, and me most of all. And the thing I feared the most was, maybe they were right.

It was hard to defend yourself when you could barely breathe past the guilt that weighed down your chest. I ignored them until their attention moved elsewhere, which I knew it shortly would. The anger was in plentiful supply and was being spread out liberally.

"I want the seventh floor. The ninth is unlucky and I won't stay there anymore," Burrom said, as the fight for domain began again. They'd been bickering between themselves nonstop about who would take what area. The stout little Fae was the only one in the room that seemed unfretted by everything else going on. All he cared about was his sleeping requirements.

"Done," Cormac answered, I think relieved to have a problem so easily fixed.

"Wait...I already set up on the seventh," Vitor said. You'd never know that Vitor and Burrom were of the same race. Vitor was the epitome of casual and refined grace, even if he was twitching more than a chipmunk on crack lately.

"Move your shit." Cormac leaned a little further in the direction of Vitor. "I said you could stay here. If you've got an issue with the accommodations...leave. That goes for all of you." He looked to Vitor, Burrom, Rogo and Adam, who was the human's representative.

Now that the shit had hit the fan, there were no secrets left to protect. All the cards were on the table, well, as far as the humans knew anyway, but this was one of the open meetings. There were still the closed meetings where the real shit went down, but no one, including myself, thought the humans were ready for that.

"We need larger food rations," Adam said, changing the subject.

"No, you don't. If your people stopped hoarding what they get and actually ate it instead, they'd be fine," Cormac said.

"They're scared," Mark defended.

"We've got enough." Cormac flipped through a few sheets of paper in front of him.

He was looking at the inventory of supplies. I knew exactly what the papers said because I had prepared them. We still had enough if we were careful.

"And when we don't?" Mark countered.

"We'll get more."

Mark dropped the subject but I wondered the same thing in my head. Cormac couldn't single handedly grow food for everyone and we had a limited amount. I took a sip out of my coffee canister filled mostly with coffee and a drop of whiskey. It was only eleven a.m. I certainly couldn't go to the straight stuff for at least a few more hours.

"What about my sister?" Vitor asked.

She's probably dead, Vitor. They all are! Even if they aren't, you won't ever see them again so they might as well be. I sank a little deeper into seat as that sentence stole the last bit of energy I had left. I banged my head against the back of the chair but it was cushioned, so it lost all effect.

If Cormac and Vitor were going to finally come to blows, then so be it. One less mouth to feed, was the way I was starting to view it. Not that I was excited about our numbers dwindling, but if you were going to be a pain in the ass, I'd kick your butt out the door for the rippers myself. There was only so much food left and I certainly didn't want to waste it on a whiner.

"What about her?" Cormac asked - it wasn't a question, it was a threat.

"We had a deal." I heard the slightest quiver in Vitor's voice. He was realizing the same thing I was noticing; this wasn't the same Cormac I knew a week ago. The Cormac of old would have beaten him to an inch of his life. This Cormac wouldn't leave an inch. I was getting the distinct impression that Cormac was shedding his civilized façade just as quickly as civilization had fallen to ruins.

"Things change." Cormac glanced at me and I got the message. It felt as if his eyes were piercing straight through to my soul. Vitor wasn't the only person that had run out of time and he wanted to make sure I understood that loud and clear.

All eyes in the room bounced back and forth between Vitor and Cormac. Even I joined the dance.

Vitor, predictable as ever, continued on. "You are a Keeper. You keep the portals, the contracts, the peace. You can't just disregard the agreements."

"Everybody here better listen up." Cormac scanned the room, meeting stare after stare. "The Lacard is the last bastion in the storm. And it belongs to me. My rules, my way. Yesterday doesn't exist. You get in the way of my survival, then you get out." He turned and looked pointedly at Vitor before he spoke his next words. "There will be no more portals, no more contracts and if you want peace, then you better be ready to fight for it."

Vitor said nothing as Cormac grabbed his stuff from the table, preparing to leave. A few feet shuffled about as Cormac walked from the room, leaving everyone else to digest his words.

"Fair enough," Burrom said in his deep gruff voice, then gathered up his people and left, presumably to the seventh floor to evict Vitor's people.

Rogo , Adam and Vitor's people that were still there, started bartering for the floors they wanted that were left. I leaned my head back again and closed my eyes. I'd get up in a minute. Right now, I couldn't move.

I sensed a shadow and I opened them to see Vitor, sitting on the edge of the table in front of me.

"He's turning into an animal." His demeanor reminded me of the lunch lady on the playground in grammar school, when the kids got a bit too rough.

"Don't care." I hadn't cared when the kids in fifth grade beat each other up, either. Cormac was acting as raw as I felt and I understood it. Vitor was reminding me of a spoiled child, who didn't realize the world had a whole lot more problems than what was in his immediate vision. It didn't help that I knew he was playing both sides, friendly to me when it suited his purpose, but just as ready to burn me at the stake when he needed a scapegoat.

"What happened to you?" Vitor furrowed his brow as he sized me up, sensing the changes in me.

His question drummed up memories of the tornados that had sprung up when we'd been flying back, and nearly ripped the plane apart. A wall of them had formed just as we had hit Montana. There had been nothing natural about them and everything terrifying.

I shook my head. "Nothing," I answered, leaving off that I didn’t want to talk about it, but he got the hint. "I'd get over there." I tilted my head toward the group on my left, who were negotiating only a few feet from us.

I stood, getting ready to exit the room. I'd rather drag my exhausted body upward than field anymore questions. "By the way, the fifth floor has the smallest square footage and, for some reason, the water pressure sucks."

I passed by the remaining people, that were picking at the scraps of square footage left, as I walked out of the room.

CHAPTER TWO

I remained upright by sheer willpower alone as I stepped into the elevator. My hand hovered over the penthouse button before I pushed the casino main floor level instead. I'd been existing on a couple of hours of sleep a night. The moment I recharged even a little, the adrenaline drove me awake again.

The doors to the casino floor slid open like the curtains being pulled back on a play about the end of the world. Huddles of people had continued to show up after we left and were still arriving by the hour, their homes destroyed. I wasn't worried about the amount of people that showed up, I was worried that there wouldn't be more. There was no way of telling how many people were left. By our current estimates, which were really no more than guesses, ninety percent of the population was gone.

Sabrina, the resident Keeper doctor, had made a makeshift office in the gift shop, right off where the main gambling floor used to be. She was tending to the people that came in and Kever was arranging sleeping accommodations. I knocked on the open door and her head swung up from the teenage girl she was tending.

"How's it going? Can I do anything to help?" I asked her. Sabrina looked as bad as the rest of us. It didn't seem like anyone slept anymore.

"It's going," she said with a shrug. "Can you hang out a minute?"

I nodded, relieved for an excuse to stop for a minute. I slumped into the chair off to the side, as I waited for her to finish stitching up a cut in the brunette girl's arm.

"Okay, Colleen, that should take care of it," Sabrina said as she stepped back and the girl stood.

I tried not to stare but I couldn't help notice the girl's huge purple eyes once she stood and looked up at me, recognition on her face. She knew who I was. The woman the humans called *The Plague*.

Sabrina laid a hand on the girl's shoulder. "Remember what I said to you. Just come to me, okay?"

I saw the girl nod and I recognized the look on her face. She'd never ask for help. Sabrina had probably dragged the girl in here practically by force.

Sabrina shut the glass door as the girl left, and sat down in the chair next to me. We had been on friendly terms before New York happened, or *the shattering,* as people were referring to it. We'd gotten a lot closer in the last week. She was just one of those people who radiated an emotional stability that you gravitated toward in times of upheaval.

"What's wrong?" I asked as she paused. We were sitting in a room with two glass walls, and even though she'd draped fabric over them to block the view, you could still see in from certain angles. Her hesitancy was making me nervous, but I made sure to school my features and not reflect any concern that would scare an onlooker.

"Some odd things are happening," she rolled her eyes, realizing what she had said sounded ridiculous. "I mean, beyond the storms and the rippers..."

The rippers were the dark grayish, lizard skinned beings that wandered the area. They had already taken out a few Keepers on our way back. They'd killed Ben within the first two days of appearing, as well as some wolves that had been making their way to the casino. No one could even count how many defenseless humans they'd gotten, or perhaps no one wanted to tally that number. I wasn't sure what was scarier about them, how *easily* they killed or *how* they killed.

"This is the thing; we all know that this is a strange new world." We both instinctively glanced through the largest gap to the group of humans congregating outside the room. "But, it's not just the world changing for some."

"What do you mean?" The purple eyes of the girl reappeared in my mind as I guessed where she was going. When did humans start having purple eyes?

"There have been a few odd things I've seen with some of them. The eyes on the girl who was just here, which I'm sure you noticed, were purple. She said her eyes used to be blue until a day ago. "

"Is there anything else?" Eye color changing was weird, but our environment had changed so perhaps not that weird. Maybe color changes were similar to getting tanned skin in a sunnier climate.

"This one is even stranger. A mother brought in her baby, who she thinks is growing a tail."

"A tail?"

She nodded. "It's just a nub but she swears it didn't used to be there. I believe her."

"How many people do we have here now?" I asked. Sabrina had been on the front lines since we left to go to New York. It didn't matter what time I came here, she was already here before me, helping someone. She saw every person that walked through those doors and was a habitual note keeper.

"My last count was three thousand humans, give or take a hundred."

"And are those the only two cases so far?"

"That I know of." The way she said it implied

she suspected more.

"Still, it's not even one percent of the population. I don't think we should worry anyone, just yet." Anyone meaning Cormac. I knew that was why she had told me. Neither of us spoke his name because then it would be an actual decision not to tell him. This way, it was just a passing conversation.

"Cormac seems to be running a little hot since you guys came back."

"That's a nice way of putting it," I told her and cemented our decision to not go directly to him with her concerns. "I've got some things to handle. Call me on the funny phone if you need me." The funny phones that ran signals through the towers Cormac had erected were the only communications left. Satellite was gone, cable gone...everything...just gone.

"You should get some sleep," she said.

"Yeah and so should you," I said with a smile; for some reason, I found it funny at that moment that neither of us would probably see a bed anytime soon. "I need to go check out the gasoline supplies. Figure out how much longer we get to keep our electricity for." I walked to the door and held it open as she joined me, walking out to fetch another human patient.

"Sounds like a plan." She straightened the stethoscope hanging around her neck as she walked past me. "I'm going to go stitch up a couple more bodies."

I watched Sabrina gather up another ravaged refugee before I headed off to the garages where the generators were housed.

I didn't like to linger on the main floor, where the humans hung out, for too long but I was detoured when a loud clap of thunder drew my attention outside. Dark stood at the main entranceway, where he was stationed. Cormac had posted men at every door, but not to keep anyone in, this time it was to keep things out.

Dark was our resident wolf adoptee who, after helping The Keepers, was persona non grata among his own. Dodd had taken him under his wing and even given him his spare bedroom. Good thing too, because it was a packed house these days.

"How long has it been doing this?" I asked as I watched softball size hail inflict even more damage to an already wrecked city.

"About an hour or so," he said, and flipped his almost feminine blond locks out of his left eye and absently petted the real wolf, Abby, who sat by his feet.

"You feel okay?" I asked, noticing his slightly flushed skin.

"I think I just ate something off. I'm fine."

I knew a brush off when I heard one and I let the subject drop. I'd heard rumors that the wolves were having a hard time holding their form, lately. Whatever it was, it was putting a serious strain on his system.

I rested my forearm on the glass of the door

and I leaned in, trying to get the best view of the area outside. The strange large cracks that ran up and around the building really looked like a moat now as they filled with water. I couldn't remember the last time Vegas had seen so much rain. For a city that normally got a little over four inches annually, we'd already met our quota for the next twenty years.

"Any sign of rippers?" I asked, knowing Dark would already be familiar with the new slang.

"No sign of anything."

"It'll be dark out, soon," I said as I watched the sky become tinged with purple.

Dark nodded. "The night crew will be on soon. Cormac upped the count to five per entrance."

There had been a few sightings of rippers in daylight, but they were overwhelmingly nocturnal creatures. Maybe they hid somewhere until nighttime, like some sort of demented vampire breed. A schedule had been set up for watches and there was always someone on during the day anyway, just in case a random one showed up on the horizon.

"You know, this isn't your fault," he said after a few minutes of silence had passed.

"Yeah, I know." And that was my cue to go. I wasn't ready for a conversation on how much of this was my responsibility. I tried to smile like I meant it as I pushed off the door, leaving Dark to finish his watch shift.

The casino was huge and it took me about ten

minutes to get to the area that housed the generators and gasoline supplies. Pat, one of the engineers on permanent staff, was already there, going over the monster machines. I'd met him several times when he had been working on fixing up the portal room, after my oopsy moments. He was Keeper-born, but a dud; what they call Keepers that don't have any abilities. I was pretty sure it was a name no one used openly, kind of how they only called me *the plague* behind my back.

"How long before lights out?" I asked as I looked at the line of gasoline containers. They looked impressive until you realized how much juice these things burned.

"At our current rate of consumption, I'd give us another week, tops," Pat said, his face showing concern.

"We need the scouting party to go further out to collect gas." All the electricity had died sometime around the time the New York tear was closed. We weren't sure if it had been the severe storms it that had kicked up at that moment, or something about the Magic that affected it, but The Lacard power had been running off a generator ever since.

Scouting parties went out during the day to retrieve any supplies they could find, but there was a limit to how far they could go and still make it back before nightfall, when the rippers came out in force.

"Even if they find some more, it'll fix us for a

while...but then what?" Pat dropped to his haunches as he tinkered with something on one of the larger generators.

He was right. The oil fields were abandoned. Refineries? Abandoned. Whatever existed now was all there would be for the foreseeable future. I'd never thought about it before, but civilization needed a certain amount of man power to keep everything running. Even if we managed to eliminate the ripper problem, we still didn't have enough bodies to drill for oil, mine for coal, man the power plants and refineries, farm food or do most of the things needed to continue the life we had taken for granted.

"Then we figure something else out," I said with much more confidence than I felt. "We do whatever we have to."

CHAPTER THREE

I couldn't remember when I finally crashed, only that I was lying in Cormac's bed in the penthouse and I didn't know how I got there. It was dark and the wind was howling outside like it did in a hurricane. And, for a split second, I forgot what the world had become. I rolled over to look out the wall of glass, expecting to see objects flying through the air with the rough winds. Instead, ten rippers hovered outside the window and reality kicked me in the gut.

My involuntary scream pierced the air. Cormac ran in the room and immediately went to the window, pulling the drapes closed.

"I'm sorry," he said after the rippers were out of view. "I forgot to close them when I brought you in here."

"It just startled me." I sat up in bed, pushing my hair out of my eyes. I looked at the clock that read one in the morning. "How did I get here?"

"You fell asleep while you were talking to Pat. He said you were leaning against the wall talking one second and then you were out, sleeping right where you stood." He walked over and stood at the foot of the bed. "Just to warn you, he's a little freaked out."

"Why?"

"You were emitting some of that white smoke stuff again while you slept. He said it was coming out of your nose when you breathed out."

"Shit." Somehow, that wasn't overly surprising to me. Everything weird happened while I slept and I had zero control over it. This pattern had caused me problems my entire life.

"You know it freaks everyone out. When you get that tired, you need to sleep." He didn't look at me when he spoke, just crossed the room and walked into the closet area.

"I didn't do it on purpose," I yelled after him, feeling like I'd just been chastised for scaring the normal people.

He walked back out and paused at the foot of the bed again. "I'm not upset that you scared Pat. I'm pissed that you're falling asleep standing up in the generator room."

"I can't remember the last time I saw you sleep." And it hit me, when had I seen him sleep? My face scrunched in what I'm sure was a very unbecoming expression. "*Do* you sleep anymore?"

"Yes. Are you hungry?"

I could still tell when someone was lying, like he was now, which was comforting. Why would he lie about sleeping? Unless he didn't need to anymore, because he was being affected by the changes as well.

"I know something's up with you." He was back in his massive closet and didn't bother to respond. The first time I'd seen the inside of it, I'd been shocked by how many pairs of black pants and white shirts the man owned. When I'd asked what the point of it was, I'd been informed that there are French cuffs, English spreads, pleats or no pleats...and my eyes had glazed over.

"Why am I in here? Do you mind explaining that?" I continued.

"It's more secure," he said as he walked out of the closet, buttoning up a fresh dress shirt. Good thing he had a large stash of them. I wasn't sure if the casino's cleaning department was as good as his normal dry cleaner, which was a pile of rubble.

"More secure? Isn't this entire place secure?" I asked, as I watched Cormac go back and adjust the drapes again.

"Yes, but this room in particular has certain protections that not even the building or the rest of the penthouse has. It's where I slept, so I made sure it was impenetrable," he said, still looking at the covered window. "I'll be rectifying that so the whole building will be just as secure, but it's big, so it takes time."

He said *slept*, not sleep. Whatever, he could

keep his secrets. I had my own that I didn't feel like sharing.

"There are a lot of the rippers tonight."

"I know."

"You think it's odd?" I asked, knowing what he was thinking or maybe just projecting my own thoughts.

He leaned a hip against the dresser and crossed his arms, keeping eye contact.

I hated when he answered without speaking. I knew what he was thinking anyway. It was my own fear that I kept trying to ignore. "It's not me."

He raised his eyebrows.

"Words, Cormac. Use your words."

"I've got to get back. I've got a meeting in the living room." He pushed off the bureau and walked out.

Meeting? I thought as I scrambled out of his massive bed. He let me sleep through a meeting? My controlling nature was *not* happy about that.

I looked around the room and saw a pair of my jeans and a shirt sitting on the dresser. I needed a shower more than anything but that would have to wait until after I found out what they were discussing. I knotted my blond hair into a bun on top of my head and went out to discover what these people were up to without me.

I suppressed my annoyance at not being awakened. I've been a worst case scenario girl my whole life. How do you *not* include me in a meeting about the end of the world? The nerve!

When I walked into the living room, it was the usual suspects. Vitor sat at the furthest point possible away from Burrom. Dark was chilling in the corner. Dodd was projecting an imposing figure, standing in the corner as a visual warning to the rest of the room to not step out of line, Buzz next to him acting as back up. Sabrina had joined the group and already appeared to be annoyed. Cormac stood front and center. He reminded me of a rock formation on a craggy shore, the waves beating against him but without affect.

And Rogo, head werewolf, was bouncing around, blustering. I had my own personal issues with him, or his people, I should say. I didn't think he had anything to do with the death of my mother, but I'd bet he knew who did. He was always at these meetings. Never missed a single one.

It was a scaled down version of earlier today but without having every underling available to hear all the gory details. These were the real meetings. This is where it got down and dirty. The humans weren't invited to these. Too many of them might panic and no one wanted to risk a mass of thousands of humans freaking out any more than they already were.

"Why should I have to have a man on every gas scout? My guys are dropping like flies," I heard Rogo complain as I took a seat next to Sabrina.

The meetings in the conference room didn't tally the dead, or decide who was the most expendable. They didn't discuss who were the most expendable people and therefore best for scouting the farthest distances, because they might not make it back in time to avoid the rippers.

"Your people can smell better than anyone in this room. That's what you bring to the table. If you aren't willing to pitch in, you're out," Cormac said in a calm voice that carried a tone of finality. We all knew *out* meant out on the street, not just the meeting. If he thought he was losing men now, those casualties would be nothing compared to losing the security of the casino and its many wards. "We're all losing people. Why should yours be any different?"

Put in that way, no one was surprised when Rogo accepted the terms. Leaving The Lacard meant certain death for them. Unbeknownst to me, The Lacard had already been enchanted a long time ago. Burrom and Cormac had been reinforcing those spells all week. The wolves had no magic, but they were unbelievable at sniffing out resources, which gave them some clout.

"What's the word on the tornados?" Burrom asked, looking to Sabrina. The best intelligence we had was from the refugees who had been traveling far and wide to get here, having heard whispers about a place untouched by the shattering. Sabrina saw the new arrivals before anyone else and possessed the most information about what they'd witnessed.

The humans also resented everyone

nonhuman right now; it was hard to blame them, too. Once the story had gotten out about how this happened, the Fae, wolves and Keepers were all equally disliked, with a special place of animosity reserved just for me. They kept most of their anger under wraps though, since they needed to stay here to survive.

Sabrina, on the other hand, had somehow escaped their wrath. I'm not sure if it was because she tended them daily and it made it harder to hate her or because she had not been with us when it had gone down and that proved her innocence. Either way, we all looked to her for information on what the humans knew.

"Besides the occasional storms popping up, from what they have heard, there is about a ten mile wide strip that runs from the panhandle of Florida diagonally up towards Seattle. No one knows how far northwest it stretches, just that tornados are constant in that strip. As soon as one dies, another takes its place. Sometimes not one, but two and three at a time."

I stood and walked over to the windows, the drapes still open. I knew Cormac only closed them for my sake. I'd realized he never closed them when he was alone. Maybe he refused to yield anything else to the rippers, or maybe he simply didn't care. They never did seem to rattle him the way they did me or the others. I couldn't know for sure because I refused to ask. That was my thing, they might scare the hell out of me, but goddamn if

I'd ever be willing to talk about it.

Looking out the window, I knew in my gut I was safe, but I still didn't get too close. They were still out there, even if I couldn't see them. They'd been hovering around the corner not even fifteen minutes ago.

Looking downward, I saw the waves crashing around the cracks that were now a moat. There was a nice chunk of land within its borders that the children played on during the day, but only when the weather wasn't going crazy and rippers weren't around.

"We need livestock. Couldn't we break up some of the cement around the building and plant grass for grazing?" It might have been a ridiculous question for all I knew about farming, but the food supplies were a constant debate lately and on everyone's mind. All the food in the refrigerators of the nearby casinos had gone bad. There were still supplies that had been scavenged from the nearby buildings but there were a lot of mouths to feed. If we didn't start to farm or do something to start producing, we'd run out.

"There isn't enough ground around the building to sustain the amount of animals we'd need, but perhaps we could offset what we have to scavenge until we figure something out," Cormac said.

Cormac walked over and looked down. "We've got to find them first." He turned back toward the group. "We need some volunteers to scout out some of the nearest farms that might still have livestock like chickens."

No one said anything but I heard a couple of groans.

"What about sending the humans?" Rogo said. "They've got to start carrying their weight."

I let out a small yelp, distracting the group from what was going to break out into the exact same argument we've had at almost every private meeting before. A ripper floated into view unexpectedly and it pissed me off that I'd just showed my hand like that. Now the whole room would know they freaked me out. No one liked them, but I was the only person who had just screamed like a sissy.

Cormac whipped back around and saw the thing hovering there, staring in. "And we need to figure out what the hell these things are," I said.

I stared at it now, refusing to be intimidated by the thing, especially with it behind a wall of glass that I was sure was impenetrable.

Images of the moment right after the plane crash came to mind. It had been right before dawn when we had staggered, one by one, from the wreck. We hadn't even seen them coming. It wasn't until we heard a scream that anybody even turned around to see a few Keepers being ripped apart by these creatures. They were torn into pieces before any of us could get to them. The creatures gone, leaving discarded body parts scattered on the ground.

They appeared more opaque now than when I had first glimpsed them, the night the plane of magic had merged into our existence. Was the magic strengthening them or was feeding on us making them more solid?

The ripper's eyes glowed in its head and its body seemed coated with a reptilian type skin. Lanky limbs, overly long for its body, and hair that cascaded almost as long. Its fingers were razor-like and I remembered the blood that had dripped from the hands of the rippers that night.

The same kind of creature that floated in front of me now had eaten our kind, not long ago. Maybe the exact same one. I stared at it and felt like the thing had eyes for me only.

Cormac stepped in between the ripper and me. The thing opened its mouth and I imagined made some sort of noise, but I couldn't hear it through the thick pane of glass. Then all I saw was Cormac's chest as he blocked its view and mine, effectively ending our standoff.

"We need to double down on our food scouts and gas scouts," Cormac said. "And I want a farm scout group sent to everything within fifty miles that might have had livestock."

"We need one more group," I stated as I gave the ripper my back as well. "Who wants to help me kill these fucking things?"

CHAPTER FOUR

Cormac stepped into my room and shut the door, planting himself in front of it. Mine was the only other bedroom of the penthouse suite.

"Where are you going?"

I'd just thrown on my black jacket. Vegas had become unseasonably cool since the change and I wanted to be as comfortable as I could if I went out tonight. When I tried to recruit a group to figure out what the rippers were, Cormac had squashed the idea before I'd even gotten a bite. That didn't mean I wasn't still planning on doing it.

"Huh? I'm not going anywhere."

"You're going to lie to me?" He stood in front of the doorway and made it clear that he would be stopping me whatever way necessary.

"I'm going to go have a chat with Burrom, if you must know my every move. I didn't think staying in the casino was going somewhere." That wasn't a lie. I did want Burrom's help.

He eyed me up and down. He stepped out of the way but placed a hand on the door just as I went to open it.

"It's not your fault. When are you going to snap out of this?"

I turned to face him. "I'm sorry if destroying the world has thrown me into a funk."

I went and pulled the door open an inch before he slammed it shut again.

"Stop being so melodramatic. It was this or extinction for them and us. They'll get over it."

"What? In a few hundred years if we haven't all been eaten alive by the rippers?" I slammed my hand against the door out of frustration. "Don't you get it? I'm not like you. I care."

"Well get over it. And you better start realizing that I'm not going to allow you to do stupid shit that endangers your life just because your head's all out of whack from misplaced guilt."

"I helped destroy their world! How is that misplaced? If I didn't think they'd be worse off without me, I'd let them rip me apart."

He inched closer until I was forced to give up some ground or have him on top of me. "You better cut this out."

"I know you don't get this. You're completely unfazed by it, but you can't scare me out of feeling guilty." My voice rose by the end of the sentence.

He backed off after I called him out on his bully tactics and took a couple of paces away from me, then turned so suddenly it caught me off guard. "Then what can I do?"

I slumped against the door, wishing he could make this horrible feeling go away. "This isn't something you can control. There's nothing you can do to fix this. You just have to give me time."

He pulled open the side of my jacket. "That's not going to fix it either," he said, motioning to the flask in my inner pocket.

"It's not like I'm stumbling around the place drunk."

"No, but when was the last day you've been completely sober either?"

I didn't say it, but I knew right off the top of my head. *New York.* I started drinking on the plane ride back and hadn't stopped.

He shook his head and left the room.

I walked out a minute later, still waiting for him to try and go all cave man on me. He didn't. He just let me go. It was probably stupid, but I suddenly was a bit annoyed. If he did think I was going to kill myself, he could've put up a bit more of a fight.

I took the stairs, even though Pat said our gas supplies were still okay. When it came to being stuck in an elevator, I decided the ease was no longer worth the risk. Better to break the habit now than to eventually be stuck.

When I got to the seventh floor, wouldn't you know that Burrom had all the entrances guarded? I was pretty sure he was trying to keep two types out, Vitor's Fae and humans. The Fae who was sitting on the stool recognized me and waved me in.

The whole floor looked radically different. The weird smoke that used to fill his bar hung heavy in the air and the lights were dimmed. I wasn't sure if Fae didn't like the bright lights or didn't need them. I still knew very little about the Fae, even though it was half my bloodline.

Most of the doors were open, as people communed in and out, which made it harder to find his room. I turned a corner and was about to ask someone when I saw a familiar shape down at the end. A short, stout figure with green highlights in his hair walked into the last unit on the end.

The door was wide open when I got there. I was about to tap on it anyway when he spoke. "Come in, Jo, and shut the door."

The room was one of the several suites located on the seventh floor and had couches, a bar area and a separate bedroom off to the side. He settled into the dark brown leather sofa as he waited for me to come in. Dressed in denim and a metal band t-shirt, he was a complete oddity.

I proceeded into the room but didn't sit. The topic on my mind might get me thrown out quickly, so I might as well not get too comfy. I'd been in close contact with Burrom for the past week and I knew there was more to his story than was being said. I didn't care about his secrets but I wasn't walking away from anyone that had knowledge.

"What brings you here?" he asked.

I'd thought about how I was going to broach the subject all yesterday. Burrom wasn't one for decorum and he detested weakness, so I decided a direct approach would give me the best shot. Or, it might insult him. I didn't think he'd kill me though, so I opted for a direct question.

"I know you're Fae, but you're not like the rest of them."

He didn't reply, just pulled out a pipe and lit the tobacco. He didn't lunge at me or kick me out, so I continued on.

"What *exactly* are you?"

"I've got a question for you," he said and then took a long puff on his pipe. "How do you know I'm not?"

I shook my head. I felt it the same way I felt the energy of a wormhole, but it wasn't something I could explain logically. "I don't, but I know I'm right."

"Sit. I'm not going to eat you," he said, puffing again on his pipe and waving his hand toward the seat next to him. "You're too old for my tastes."

I sat, hoping his last line had been a joke.

"What are you?" I asked again.

"Tell me why you want to know."

I didn't want to explain the silver smoke that crept around me and was now coming out of me, but if I wanted information, I was going to have to take a leap of faith and trust him.

"You know about the silver strands, you've

seen them first hand."

He didn't speak, just nodded.

"They're coming out of me now."

He cocked his head to the side, squinting his narrow eyes even smaller. "How?"

I let out a deep breath as I resigned myself to having to get into the nitty gritty details. "It happens when I'm sleeping, so I haven't seen it myself. I'm told that it starts to seep out of my nose and mouth while I'm sleeping. Not as dense as the strands you've seen, more of a wispy nature."

He sat there, just taking it all in, as he watched me.

He took another puff on his pipe and I suppressed the urge to choke on the smoke.

"I'm going to share some things with you."

"Okay," I said, wondering what the delay was.

"This can't be repeated. If you do repeat it...I'll kill you."

I nodded. He would, too. I could tell from the way he ran his affairs. You didn't cross Burrom.

"And I want something in return."

Nothing surprising there. "What?"

"Protection."

That was surprising. What would he need protection from, that I could provide better than him?

"My time is coming and when it does, I'll be vulnerable, more so now than ever. I will help you, but in return, you will do this for me." He pointed at me with his curvy handled pipe.

"What time? And how am I going to protect you?" I didn't like to show my weaknesses, but this screamed for a large dose of reality.

He just smiled. "If I'm right, I have no doubt in your ability to do so."

I tried to think this over the best I could. Once he started spilling whatever information he had, there'd be no turning back. "Will I have to hurt anyone?"

"No."

Quick firm answer, off to a good start. "Nothing morally objectionable?"

"No."

"To my moral standards, not yours." Insulting, but it had to be qualified.

He laughed a little. "No. Don't you trust me, Jo?" he asked in a mocking tone.

"Then okay."

He held out his stumpy hand and I accepted it, hoping he wouldn't do any funny charm or spell on me.

"I'm a Ground Fae."

"What is that?"

"You wouldn't know because there are only five of us left in existence. I live above ground for several hundred years and then I hibernate for another fifty, underground, before emerging once again in a different form."

I started to suspect he was much older than I'd ever imagined. "I thought Fae only lived about five hundred years."

"Vitor's kind do. But I'm of an altogether different breed."

I nodded, still not understanding the need for such secrecy.

"When I go underground, that is when I'll need you. These are scary times, and not because of what you think. I originated here on Earth, way back at the dawn of creation. Back when magic was stronger, but still nothing like this."

"So, then you have an idea of what is going on?"

"It's not the same as then. At that time, there was more magic but everything was in balance. Now it's different."

"How so?"

"Because magic was never meant to exist in this strength. It's like rain. You get different amounts every year, but within a certain range. This is like a magic tsunami."

"Do you know what the smoke is?"

"It's a pure form of magic."

Goosebomps spread out across my skin as his words cemented in my brain.

"And the dark smoke the senator used against me?" I asked, already having my own hunch.

"Magic that has been twisted," Burrom confirmed.

"The smoke that has been seeping out of me, I don't know where it comes from. I used to only see it, but now..." I couldn't say it again, as my palms grew sweaty at the thought.

"I think as the magic grows stronger..."

"Stronger? You think it's still accumulating?"

"Yes, I do. And I think as it does, it's building up in your body more."

"Do you think I could get rid of it?"

"I don't think so, but I don't know why you'd want to. And if there was a way, I wouldn't tell you, anyhow. I need you to use it."

"But I don't know how to do that, either." I looked to him, hoping he was going to explain that next.

He just shook his head. "No idea. I don't even know if I'm correct, but I believe I am. And if it is the case, we both need you to figure out how."

"I still don't know why you need me?"

"Because when I go to ground, I need you to seal my place of resting."

"What did you used to do?"

"We used to help protect each other, but as our numbers dropped, it became more difficult. There were more of us a long time ago, but we've lost many because of killings during hibernation."

My funny phone buzzed on the seat next to me and I looked down and saw Sabrina's name flash on the screen. Worst timing ever, but it had to be important. She rarely called me. There wasn't a need, when I saw her every day.

"Go ahead," Burrom said, seeing my expression.

I grabbed my phone and walked to the other side of the room. I was still in earshot so I wasn't sure what the point was.

"Everything okay?" I asked her.

"Do you know someone named Oslo? He's down here asking for you."

I bit my lip.

"What's he look like?" Let him be blond and short.

"Tall, lean but muscular, black hair and very pale skin."

I shouldn't have been surprised but I was anyway. Oslo was a crafty character. I'd started my new life with ID and documents purchased from him. We'd met when I was a teenager, selling fenced goods and hot cars to him. The last time I'd talked to him, I had used him to send Cormac on a wild goose chase. Now he was here. Brilliant.

I told Sabrina I'd be down in five minutes, hung up the phone and turned to Burrom. "I've got to go."

His short frame rose from the couch to his full height, just shy of five feet and I thought he was going to give me a hard time about leaving. That wasn't his purpose at all.

"You repeat what I've told you to no one."

I looked down at the small Fae and really saw why the other Fae cowed to him. There was something a bit crazy behind those eyes, when they stared at you. I got the feeling that not only would he kill me if I said something, he might really eat me, like he implied earlier.

"Not a word," I said and meant it. I did not

intend to screw with this particular Fae. "We'll finish this conversation soon."

CHAPTER FIVE

I left the room and practically ran down the hall and into the elevator. I didn't have time for the stairs. I needed to get Oslo out of here, and pronto. If I couldn't get him out of here, I'd at minimum make sure he was going to keep his silence.

The ground floor was crawling with humans when I got there. I dodged in between them as I made my way to Sabrina's office, trying to pretend I didn't see the glares. My throat constricted when I saw it was indeed Oslo. Worse, Cormac was in the room as well. This was not looking good. I wanted to sprint the last fifty feet to them but that would scream guilt.

When I got to the door, everyone turned to me. Sabrina mouthed sorry and rolled her eyes toward Cormac, making it clear that she hadn't been the one who had called him here.

"Jo," Oslo greeted me.

At least he was calling me Jo, the name I'd assumed as an adult. That was a positive sign.

Cormac tilted his head in Oslo's direction. "Your *friend* has a message for you that he refused to share until you were present." Cormac didn't like that many people. If he had been Santa, there would be a whole lot of coal going around. It looked like Oslo had made the naughty list.

"Can we go somewhere more private?" Oslo asked, looking around at the glass walls. "This might not be something you want to go public with."

My stomach clenched and my eyes darted around the room. I wasn't sure I wanted to go private with whatever it was, either. I'd prefer if it just went away altogether, but that didn't appear to be an option.

"Sure. Come on." I led him out of Sabrina's office and headed toward the conference room upstairs, hoping it was empty. I turned back in the guise of making sure Oslo was following me. How full of it was I? I really wanted to see if Cormac was. He was following right behind Olso, like a dark shadow of death just waiting to strike.

Now what? Cormac knew I had a shaded past. I was prepared for that skeleton. The goose chase I'd sent Cormac on with Oslo's help? That haunting seemed imminently close, with the ghost right on my tail.

I'd stay close to Oslo. If I had to take him down to keep him quiet, I would. I'd apologize in a note pinned to his shirt when he woke up tomorrow, miles away from here.

"Long time since I saw you in class. How have you been faring in these crazy times?" Oslo asked.

I inwardly sighed in relief. He was letting me know he wasn't here to give me up. But if he's not here to blackmail me or some other such thing, what the hell did he want? His clothes and appearance didn't look like he'd been toughing it out, so he wasn't a refugee seeking shelter.

"As good as can be expected. How about..." My feet flew up over my head and I knew I was in for one dozy of a headache as I was about to land head first. I felt Cormac's hands on my arms right before I totally wiped out.

"What did I slip on?" I asked as Cormac helped me right myself. I looked down and there was a four feet by four feet area of carpet gone with stone in its place.

"What happened to the floor?" I asked, looking at the weird spot. "Renovations? Now?"

"I'll ask Dodd," Cormac said.

He held the door to the conference room open for us and just as Oslo was about to follow him in, I saw Dodd and Buzz turn the corner down the hall. I held back a sigh of annoyance. Of course, they would run right over.

Oslo stopped a couple feet inside the room and I knew what was running through his mind.

"You'll get safe passage out of here," I said, then threw him a look that made it clear, as long as he didn't screw with my secrets. Oslo was slick enough to get the point and gave a subtle single nod.

"What about them?" Oslo asked, looking over at the three menacing figures, also known as Cormac, Dodd and Buzz.

"Cormac?"

He stared down Oslo for a minute. "This is a one-time offer."

"That's all I need," he said. Oslo sized up the room before he turned back and looked at me. "I'm here on behalf of the senator." It was telling that in a room full of chairs, not one person sat.

Of all the things he could have said, that was the last thing I expected. Buzz edged in closer to Oslo, Dodd silently positioned himself next to the door and Cormac moved nearer to me. It was weird, like they'd been practicing. Strange men, they might have been too. If they had, I was glad I *hadn't* been invited, for once.

"Frisk him," Cormac told Buzz, probably thinking what I was. Rick. Promises and assurances wouldn't do us any good if he had no control of himself. The image of Rick shooting a bullet into his own head would never leave me.

Oslo stepped back from the table and raised his hands in compliance as Buzz patted him down.

"He's clean," Buzz said and returned to his spot by the door.

"I understand your concern but I'm not corrupted. I never come into physical contact with him."

"Is that how it happens?" I asked.

"Yes. He's got a way of interjecting a piece of himself into people with touch. But I'm pretty sure he doesn't like to do it."

"Why are you here?" I asked.

"To offer you his terms of peace."

"Terms?" Cormac scoffed.

"Yes," Oslo continued looking at me. "The senator wants to offer you a deal."

"After our last encounter, what makes him think I'd even negotiate? He's the one that ran, not me."

Oslo's eyes widened slightly at that. I didn't add that I'd very nearly died and my control over the silver strands was nonexistent.

"That's your decision, but I have to deliver the terms. That's on me." He said it like a man that knew what the consequences of not fulfilling his responsibilities were.

"Go ahead," I said.

"Are you familiar with the wall of tornados that are running diagonally through North America?" Oslo continued.

"Yes, we're aware of them," I replied.

"They extend all the way around the Earth."

And it just gets better and better. Wait until the crowd downstairs hears about this one. Wow, is my popularity going to skyrocket then.

Oslo walked to where there was an antique globe in the corner and traced a line with his finger, demonstrating the divide all the way to China.

"The senator has agreed to relinquish any claim on this side of the globe," he pointed to the half we were in, "if you stay out of his half."

I had no honor left when it came to the senator. I wouldn't handicap myself to rules I doubted he'd adhere to. What did I care if I said yes now and then backed out on the deal? But the senator would expect this, so instead of jumping the gun, I waited for the other shoe to drop.

"And?"

Oslo smiled slightly, reminding me of the person I used to know before the world had turned on its ear. Once he'd declared himself as the senator's man, it was startling how quickly he'd changed in my eyes, evidenced by this slight reminder of who he used to be.

"We will need reassurances, of course," he finally said.

"Of course," Dodd said in the background.

"Which are?" I asked. Cormac remained silent. Oslo might not know it, but that was worse than threats.

"I have a list of people I am to return with, if you agree."

That would never happen, but I held my cards close to my chest. My entire life had become a poker metaphor. I really needed to stop gambling. Good thing the casino floor was filled with refugees instead of gamblers. "So, what do we get?"

"You get peace."

I stood on the opposite side of the table and waited for the rest of it, but got nothing. "You've told us the stick, no carrot? You can't expect us to take an offer of peace with nothing to back up the gesture." No one in the room would accept the deal anyway, but it would be good to know what they had to offer.

"We can also tell you how to kill the things you call rippers."

And that was their ace in the hole. How to neutralize the rippers was a game changer. We could send out scouts without the threat of death or simply being able to walk outside the casino at night without constant fear.

I stepped back and looked at Cormac, Dodd and Buzz to see their reactions. It was pointless. Even Buzz was unreadable today. Must have been those secret practices.

"If you would be inclined to offer me lodgings, I've got two days before I need to return with your answer."

"Leave your list and we'll think it over. Buzz will get you a room," Cormac said.

Oslo reached into his back pants pocket and laid a folded sheet of paper on the table.

I watched his cold manner. I knew he'd come up rough, much like me, but it didn't squash the anger I felt. "Is it worth it? Whatever you are getting to work with a killer?" I asked, having a hard time not viewing this as a betrayal to the human race.

"I don't know. Is it?" he asked, then looked at Cormac.

"Not even close to the same."

"We all have our lies that let help us go on," Oslo replied.

"Out," Cormac said in a barely restrained voice. "My promise was to let you leave here alive. I didn't promise how long you'd make it after you left."

Oslo didn't utter another word and turned toward the door.

I finally sat down as I watched Buzz escort him out. The sound proofed door slid shut with a click, leaving Cormac, Dodd and me alone in the room.

"The senator has at least one person inside here," Dodd said, speaking first.

"I agree. He's got spies," I said. "That's not surprising, with the amount of people we've taken in. That'll be handled. Right now, I want to know who's on the list."

I grabbed a pencil from the sideboard and used the eraser to drag it over, skeptical of touching it.

The only thing on the sheet was a list of ten names. I recognized most of them as humans that I'd had limited contact with, but my heart gave an extra beat when I saw the name on the bottom. As soon as I felt my reaction to seeing Sabrina on the list, I realized a tiny part of me had been considering the deal.

"We can't do it." I pushed the paper away, annoyed with myself. Realizing who I was starting to become made me that much more opposed, as my conscience needed the salve to my guilt.

Cormac leaned over the table and looked down at the sheet. He stood back and didn't say a word.

"What is it?" Dodd asked and then looked at the sheet himself. "Absolutely not. Why the hell would they even want her?"

"Relax, it's not happening," Cormac said.

The door swung open and we all turned to see Buzz walking in with Sabrina herself behind him.

"Kever is showing Oslo to his room," Buzz said.

I looked at her and couldn't help wondering why the senator would've wanted her. It didn't make any sense to me. Nothing about the list was clicking into place.

"Why are you all looking at me oddly?" Sabrina asked.

I looked away quickly, with everyone else. I guess we were all wondering the same thing.

"What is it?" she asked again.

One of us must have looked to the sheet on the table, or maybe the single sheet just lying there by itself was tip off enough, because she made a grab for it. Dodd lunged at it too, but a split second too late.

"What is this and why is my name on it?" She looked at each of us and I felt even worse as her eyes came to rest on me, like she expected me to be the one to be honest with her.

"That came from the senator. I'm not sure you

should touch it," I finally said.

"What is it? Why is my name on a list from the senator?" she asked, ignoring my advice, still gripping the sheet.

Dodd spoke then and told her of Oslo's demands from the senator.

As he spoke, I watched her reaction go from outrage, to anger and finally defeat within the course of a few minutes. She sank into the conference chair, her normally perfect posture abandoned for the slouch of resignation.

"I should go," she said.

"You are not going!" Dodd exploded as he watched her whole demeanor become resigned.

She ignored him, looking completely dejected.

"You aren't going," Cormac said, backing up Dodd.

"Maybe I should," she said.

"What are you saying?" Dodd demanded. "Absolutely not!"

"Why these people?" I asked, looking at the list again.

"I think I might know," Sabrina answered. "Remember what we were talking about the other day?" she asked as she turned to me.

"Yes," I said, thinking back to the humans who were mutating and the story she told me about the baby with the tail.

Sabrina caught Cormac, Dodd and Buzz up to speed on what she had witnessed with the humans.

"Every name on this list is a human that's changing," she explained to us.

"But why are you on it?" I asked.

She stood up and raised her shirt, baring her stomach where patches of blue scales were forming in an irregular pattern that was about two inches wide.

"Why didn't you say anything?" I was stunned by the sight of the scales forming on her skin.

"I'd been running so crazy I hadn't even noticed. I thought it was rough skin at first and it's not like I've had time to preen in the mirror. I didn't notice it was actually scales forming until today, when one of them actually flaked off into my hand." She pulled her shirt down and collapsed back into the chair.

"But if you didn't know, how would the senator?" I asked. "Did you tell anyone?"

"No, I told no one. I have no idea but it's too much of a coincidence to be anything else. Every name on that list has something going on."

I leaned back, agreeing with her. Whoever the senator planted here knew things about us that we didn't even know ourselves. The thought of someone I didn't know aware of what was going on with me, and worse, maybe how to control it, was beyond frightening. Maybe it wouldn't be as alarming if I wasn't leaking smoke out my body like someone with a pack a day habit.

I reached my hand down to where my flask was tucked into my boot but I didn't pull it out.

Cormac was watching too closely and I didn't feel like hearing it. I wanted to scream at him that some people hadn't lived thousands of years and we still had emotions left. Some of us still had nerves.

"If we don't go," Sabrina continued, "it's not just about war. If we can't control the rippers, we can't farm or develop a sustainable food supply. Eventually, we'll starve to death."

"No," I said. "If he knows how to kill them then we can figure it out, too." I thought I sounded pretty tough for someone whose mouth was watering for a sip of whiskey. Someone once told me to "fake it til you make it." I couldn't believe I was following that crappy advice now. Good thing I wasn't a surgeon, or I'd be faking it all the way to the morgue.

"But how long will it take before we exhaust the supplies of the area within our range?" Sabrina said.

I didn't want to answer and Cormac was suspiciously quiet.

Dodd stormed from the room, slamming the door on his way out.

I pulled my chair closer to Sabrina. "You don't need to do this. No one is asking you to."

"We don't give up our own," Cormac said from his position on the other side of the room, squashing any discussion of it. "We've got two days to figure this out. No one says or does anything for now."

I looked back to Sabrina. "I agree with Cormac.

We'll figure something else out."

She nodded but her skin was pale and clammy looking. "I've got to get back downstairs."

A bad feeling was taking root as I watched her leave the room, Buzz exiting behind her.

Cormac came and stood next to me. "The senator knows you aren't ready to take him on, but he's not ready to take you on, either. Not with those silver strands that are popping up that can tear him to pieces."

"You mean the things I haven't seen since New York?" I asked.

"Come on. I want to show you something," he said, taking my hand.

"What?" I asked, looking at him.

"You'll like it."

CHAPTER SIX

"Should we be going up there? It's getting late," I said as we climbed the steps to the rooftop. It had once been a beautiful place and I was afraid to see what had become of it.

"Trust me."

When he opened the door, I didn't know what to expect but it wasn't anything good.

"How did you do this? And is it safe? It's going to be dark soon." It wasn't perfect. The old willow tree that had taken up one corner was gone, but the bench that sat beneath it was still there. A new tree had been planted in its place. A lot of the plants had seen better days but it wasn't horrible either. There were new flowers planted here and there and the ones left would rebound eventually. With the sun setting, off in the distance, it was almost nice again. I mean, you had to force your eyes out of focus a bit to disguise the crumbling city surrounding us, but hey, we had apocalyptic standards these days. It was like walking into a house with five kids during the summertime, you had to adjust your expectations.

"It's warded. No rippers, or anything else that might show up, can get within twenty feet."

I walked around on the grass, not realizing until right now just how desperately I missed being outside. "And there's no way to do a spell on people?"

"No. The spell has to be grounded to the earth."

I wandered around the rooftop for a few minutes before I finally got up the nerve to go as close to the edge as my fear of heights would allow. I didn't want to look but I couldn't seem to help myself. Even with the light fading, the destruction of the city was startling to the senses from this vantage point.

I sensed Cormac come up behind me.

"I'm still having a hard time believing it. I keep thinking that I'm going to look out and it will all be here like it was for as long as I've been alive." I looked up at the sky, trying to focus on something pretty and not destroyed, but even that looked off. The colors were too vivid to be normal. "Our world is gone for good, isn't it?"

"Different, not gone," he said and I felt his finger trail along the length of my spine. "I've seen a lot of change in my life. Some good, some bad...but the world adapts and moves on."

"I guess I just never thought I would see so much in my..." I started to lose my concentration. I forgot what I was going to say as he moved my hair away from the back of my neck and I felt his lips caress the sensitive skin. It was like he instinctively knew all my buttons. "Cormac..."

"Yes?" he replied, his voice deep and husky. His arm circled me and pulled me flush against him as his lips worked their way along the tendon that ran to the base of my neck.

"The contract. You have to get rid of the contract."

He took my lobe into his mouth, sucking and tenderly biting. "Why?"

His breath against my ear sent a shiver through me.

"Because I'm too young to be married." But I'm so overdue for this. I needed this.

"Contract or not, you're mine." His arm pulled me a bit firmer into him as if to prove his point.

I wanted to melt into him but logic kept niggling at my brain. End of the world logic dictated I should have sex because, I mean hey, people were dropping like flies and I deserved some hot sex before I kicked it. But marry? Was there even a divorce process with a magical marriage?

I pulled out of his arms even though my libido was screaming in protest the whole time.

"I want the contract destroyed. Vitor isn't an issue, anymore. He's powerless under the circumstances." I turned to look at him. Cormac was a guy. He wouldn't care as long as he was getting sex, right?

"So let me see if I understand this, you're willing to sleep with me but commitment is out of the question?"

He took a step back and stared at me like I was an alien being. Yeah, no sex tonight. Not the way he was looking at me.

"Why is that so bad? From what I've heard, you've screwed half the employees at The Lacard and you didn't marry them. I can't walk down a hallway without seeing a pretty girl and knowing there's a fifty-fifty shot that you slept with her." Did I just sound jealous? Ugh.

He stood there, shaking his head. "Maybe because I've been around longer then you can imagine. *Dated* all those women and I finally find one I want and she says she's only ready for sex." He turned and walked a few more feet away from me then turned back around, rubbing his jaw. "Do you know how many women want this kind of commitment from me?"

"I'm not saying I won't want it, I just want to go slower. Why do we have to move at top speed?"

"Because when you know something is right, you don't need weeks and months to figure it out." He took a couple of steps back toward me. "That's the problem. I know. You don't."

His last words filled me with nerves but I wasn't being unreasonable. "Why does wanting to move a little slower have to be such a big deal?"

He nodded, going blank and unreadable. "Fine," he finally said, then turned and left me standing on the rooftop alone, wondering what the hell "fine" meant.

CHAPTER SEVEN

The weather was crystal clear for a change and I could see a crew bashing through the cement surrounding the casino below as I stood on the roof a day later. Even if for no other reason, it would be nice for the kids to have a playground of some sort.

Oslo had been on the floors below, circulating the casino like a visiting V.P. while Sabrina was acting stranger than ever. We had a day left to figure out what to do. Cormac had already made up his mind. To him, there was no decision. Sabrina was one of his kind, and if that hadn't been enough, it would kill Dodd. Cormac was non-negotiable in that area.

What bugged me was what if it had been a list of only humans? Then what would Cormac have done? What might I have done? Problem was, I had a pretty good idea on both counts and I wasn't feeling too good about it. But that wasn't the situation and we still had a problem.

In one day, we'd send Olso packing with no living insurance of any kind. I agreed with the decision but it didn't make me feel good about what might come. In the current state, it was very hard to try and rebuild anything. A truce, even a fake one that might not last long, did have a lure.

"Are you ready?" Burrom's deep raspy voice asked as he came up beside me. We'd agreed to meet here on the roof at dusk.

"Ready for what, exactly?" His offer of help hadn't come with many details.

"To see what you've got. Cause if we can't get that juice you have inside you cranking, I'm screwed as badly as the rest of you."

"What do you have in mind?"

"Come on. I'll show you," he said and turned on his heel.

"What happens when you go underground?" I asked as I followed him downstairs and then to the abandoned service stairs that most people didn't travel. I thought I was the only one that used them until now.

"I become reborn."

"But do you die?"

"I don't know what happens during that time. I go to sleep, and when I wake, I have a new body." He exited the stairwell on the casino level and headed toward the back of the casino. Walking through the kitchens, where the humans weren't allowed, we walked toward a door guarded by Fae.

Burrom obviously knew the best way to not be seen leaving. They simply nodded as we passed through it and left.

The door opened out onto the back of the casino where a make shift ramp had been placed over the moat that circled the entire casino.

The door closed behind us and I looked up at the sky. Only a sliver of light was left.

"Burrom, are you sure about this?"

"I've got a hunch," he said, walking off and assuming I'd follow.

"A hunch isn't very reassuring," I said but followed anyway.

"Don't worry about it. I can keep the rippers off the both of us if I need to. I'm hoping I don't have to."

"If you can keep the rippers at bay, how come you aren't going out with the squads?"

His face looked affronted at the question. "I don't 'go out with squads'" he repeated in a disgusted tone. "Now, back to the subject at hand. If this senator helped your mother conceive with the help of magic, you should have the juice to as well. I'll show you how it's done and then you follow."

"Why can't you show everyone how to do it?"

"Because it's all about the juice, my dear, not enough or not the right kind and it won't work. The magic that is ruling now is the same magic you and I possess."

This was the first time since we'd come back

from New York that I'd gone further than the moat. Somehow, the moat had become the line of demarcation between safety and everything else that went bump in the night.

The streets were a disaster. Debris was everywhere, shed from the skeleton of crumpled buildings. I thought back to pictures of war torn cities that had been bombed. Pictures didn't do justice to the reality.

There are a couple types of quiet in life. The first is the peaceful dead of night when everyone is safe and sound in their beds or snowstorms, when everyone is nestled by fireplaces. Then there is this type. It's the kind I'd never experienced before where everyone is gone, the palette of voices and noise quieted in the wake of some unspeakable tragedy.

Every so often, I'd smell a whiff of smoke from some fire that was still burning out in the distance. Sometimes, I'd catch the scent of something much worse. A smell that made my eyes water and the bile churn in my stomach and I knew it was decay of a kind I didn't want to see.

We walked further from the safety of the casino and with each step, I became more and more concerned that I was making an error in judgment. I really couldn't afford any more of those. Fucking up the universe had seriously set me back. I might have maxed out my young and stupid allotment for the year.

"You're going to get me back alive, right?"

"I told you, I need you. More specifically, I need what you are capable of. From what I've heard of your past actions, I'd say I'm more invested in your well-being than you are." The little man had the nerve to laugh at his bad joke.

We finally stopped about a mile away from The Lacard, next to a crumbling building that was once one of the greatest casinos on the strip. Burrom started climbing through the rubble and into a gaping hole in the wall.

"In there? The place looks like it's going to fall down around our ears at any moment." A chunk of concrete fell a foot from where he walked just as I spoke and made my case.

"It'll be fine," he said as he dusted debris off his shoulder.

"I don't know." I looked around at what was left of the structure. The few windows that remained were nothing but uneven shards of glass.

He waited just inside the ruins and tapped his foot impatiently. "My survival is linked to yours. If I can't get you up to snuff before I go underground, then I'll be dead as well."

It was a convincing argument. "Okay, little guy, you got me," I said as I climbed over the debris to join him. He stood there, eyes squinty and brow furrowed, obviously insulted by my "little guy" comment. "Oh, come on, it was a joke."

He snorted. "Are you ready to learn?"

"Yes." I climbed past turned over slot machines, with coins spilled all over the floor.

Money was worthless, even coins had no value. Food and guns were the only currency that counted.

"You're half Fae, so you should be able to pick up on this stuff pretty quick, even if it is a less preferable bloodline. It's not like you're Ground Fae quality, but it should be enough." He made a face, as if he'd just tasted a mediocre glass of wine. One he'd make do with for the meal, but wouldn't order again. I wasn't insulted. I was just glad there was wine.

"I thought the Fae gene was suppressed when mixed with a Keeper?"

"Did a Fae tell you that?" he asked but didn't wait for an answer. "If you want to know how to make a cupcake, you ask a baker, not a mason." He pointed his short stubby little finger at me as he talked and I looked at his t-shirt. I never would have pegged him as a Guns and Roses fan.

I thought back as I watched him walk further in to the old casino and realized that all my information on being half Fae came from other sources and shook my head.

"The Fae have a vested interest in *not* letting other species have control of our abilities. We *don't* advertise. A half Fae with no training would be inept and easily help us perpetuate the lie. Your Keepers think you are so good at wormholes because of them, but you've already been using your Fae abilities."

He raised his hands, looked up and around.

"We commune with the environment, unlike normal humans. That's why you can manipulate the wormholes better than any of them."

I nodded, not wanting to cut him off, but the place was getting darker by the second. So far, this was all stuff he could've told me back at the casino. "Can we get to the good stuff now? I know you think I'm this big risk taker, bring on the danger girl, but I'm not really feeling death today." Geez, you do a couple of crazy things and they all think you're down for anything.

"Give me your hand," he said as he walked back over to me.

"Why?"

"Jo, don't you trust me?"

"No, not completely," I said and held my hand out of reach.

"Because I'm going to try and cut a few corners and jump start your system."

He tried to grab my hand again and I stepped out of reach.

"Like a broken car?"

"Yes. Pretty much."

"Could it kill me?"

"No."

I held out my hands. "What am I going to feel?"

He took them but didn't answer.

"I hope I'm at least a used Porsche. I'd hate to be a broken down...Ow." The jolt he sent through me had my fingers tingling and I felt my heart flutter in my throat. A puff of silver smoke burst from my nose.

"This *is* creepy," I said, realizing why Pat had been freaked out.

"How do you feel?" Burrom asked.

"Tingly."

"Try and control the silver smoke leaking out of you."

I focused on the wisps that lingered up and then disappeared like steam into the atmosphere.

"And try to hurry up about it, too" he said.

I looked at Burrom and just shook my head. "Goddamn rippers are coming in behind me, aren't they?"

He shrugged in a nonchalant, "you knew they would be," sort of way.

"And this is your idea of helping?"

"I told you, I can get us out of here, but I'd prefer you tried."

I turned, dreading the horrible view I was about to see. I hated the things even when I was safely ensconced in the casino, never mind standing next to them among the rubble. Three of them were gliding toward us, with Burrom at my back and me front and center.

"Can't you at least walk?" I said to the rippers, knowing that it was stupid on so many levels. They probably had no idea what I was saying, and if they did, I probably just annoyed them. But watching them glide freaked me out.

"Where is your magic going?" Burrom asked

from behind me as the silver smoke was dissipating rapidly.

The creatures edged closer, slowing with their approach.

"I don't know. Can you give me another jump?"

"No. Only if you change your mind about dying today. I told you, I can get us back but I want to see if you can fend off the rippers on your own. If you can't, you aren't as strong as I'd hoped."

The things were edging closer and closer. They stopped about three feet in front of me and stared at me, similar to how I imagined I was looking at them, like a monster exhibit at a freak show.

"Burrom?" I asked, wanting to ascertain his approximate position behind me.

"Yeah?" he replied sounding like he was about two feet behind me.

"You've got this covered, right? Because my magic seems to be failing."

"Why are they are looking at you like that?" he replied, not answering my question.

The rippers started to circle around us now, but it was me they kept their eyes on. I would have turned with them but they took different directions, making it impossible to keep them all in my line of sight.

"Are they getting ready to attack?" I asked.

"They seem fascinated by you."

"Is that a yes or a no on the attack?"

"Probably not?"

I didn't think so either, but what were they doing? And then, I looked up at the crumbled entranceway we came through and I saw more of them. It was hard to tell how many as they filtered in through the gap, but they just kept coming and coming...and coming.

"Practice is over," Burrom said, now sounding like he was inches from me.

"Ya think?" I replied. "You can handle this, right?"

"Depends on how many more show up."

"You didn't tell me there were caveats."

"In life, when aren't there?"

"So what should we do?"

"I'm not sure. I can get us out of here, but the more that come at us, the harder it is. I'm pretty sure they aren't going to like the taste of Ground Fae. Not so sure about pretty little blond Keepers."

"How many more can you handle before this is a problem?" I looked around the room doing a quick count of about fifty rippers.

"Not sure."

"Guess."

"About twenty ago."

"Then why are we standing here?"

"I've never seen such a large cluster before. Who knew?"

I watched as they slowly formed a circle around us but never came within more than three feet of me. They edged slightly closer to Burrom. *Here goes nothing,* I thought as I shuffled just a hair forward. As I'd hoped, the entire circle around me rearranged itself to my new position.

"That was interesting," Burrom said, keeping pace with me.

"Are you doing anything?" I asked.

"Not a thing. I was figuring I'd save it up in case we had to do a mad dash out of here."

"Just stay by me. I'm going to try and make up some more ground." Slowly, I continued forward. Every step I took, the group of rippers rearranged itself around us. I stepped, they stepped.

By time I made it to the door, I was taking normal steps. They didn't leave, but they kept a uniform distance from me.

"What is going on here?" I asked Burrom, as we slowly made our way back to the casino. Slowly because I wasn't ready to try out a jog yet and risk bumping into one of them.

"I don't know, but I'm not feeling anger from them, or even aggression," Burrom said as he walked next to me.

"I know," I agreed looking around at them and then straight ahead.

The Lacard hovered behind them and the real panic set in. There would be no way of getting into the casino unseen now. Cormac wasn't my worry. He'd be annoyed with me, but when wasn't he? My fear was how all the humans, who distrusted me on a good day and hated me most others, would feel.

The front door was the closest entranceway. I

was pretty sure taking this large a group of monsters around to the back entrance wasn't going to do much good so I kept plowing ahead.

There was a large group of people standing at the front doors as we approached. Cormac was front and center, with Dodd and Buzz on either side. Sabrina was on Dodd's left.

Looking at their faces, I could only imagine how bizarre a picture I must have presented. Buzz looked shocked, Sabrina concerned and Dodd might have been suppressing laughter. Cormac was stone faced, which meant he was beyond pissed off.

The humans behind them looked like an angry mob who were preparing for a witch-hunt.

I climbed the stairs to enter the casino and the rippers parted to the side as we got closer, not able to get within twenty feet because of the wards surrounding the casino.

Cormac opened the door as we approached. "Do you *ever* stop and think about what you are doing? Ever? Just once would be nice," he said in a low voice as I passed by him, entering the building.

I didn't bother replying. Cormac wasn't my concern, the angry looking crowd was. I lifted my head, refusing to cower and took a few steps toward the elevator that would lead me to the penthouse, before the crowd erupted into an angry chant. "Traitor" they started to say in unison.

They already thought I had ruined the Earth. Seeing these creatures following me was the last straw for them. I understood how bad it looked. My intentions had been good but I'd had a hand in everything that went down. I couldn't even say they were wrong in their presumptions.

Their angry glares followed me as I walked and their chanting quickly escalated to screaming. I wondered if they were about to try and rip me limb from limb, like I knew they wanted to.

"Shut up or get out!" Cormac's shout was so loud it was easily heard, even over the crowd. As quick as that, silence once again fell over the lobby of the casino. "Next person that says anything to her will be kicked out immediately."

The anger still roiled but they were silent about it now, as I decided to change my course and head to the stairway, trying to keep my composure intact. The second the door closed, I leaned against the wall and let myself fall apart.

CHAPTER EIGHT

I'd barely gotten back to the penthouse when I heard Cormac hot on my heels and the door shutting a little more loudly than normal.

"What the hell was that?" he asked as he stepped into the room a second later.

I was taken aback for a second at the sight of him in jeans. I hadn't noticed that downstairs but I'd been a bit distracted.

"Burrom was trying to help me, and it went a wee bit awry."

"You think this is funny?"

Nothing about this was funny. I'd just gotten my shaking under control a second ago. I wasn't planning to share how scared out of my wits I'd been and add fuel to the already blazing fire.

He took a couple of more steps into the room, stopping several feet shy of me. Crossed his arms in front of his chest and incline his head toward me.

"Burrom was helping you? You're going to have to expand on that. There are so many issues with that statement, I don't even know where to begin."

"He thinks he can help me out with the silver stuff."

"Again, problem. Burrom doesn't help out anybody for free. What did you agree to? And don't lie because I know it was something. Do you even know who you are negotiating with? He's a goddamn Ground Fae!"

"You knew?"

"What did you agree to?"

"I can't tell you."

He didn't press me any further, just shook his head and pulled out his phone. "Is Burrom still down there?"

I watched as he waited on the phone a moment.

"Tell him I need him in the penthouse, now. No, just him. You guys make sure the civilians stay in line and keep an eye on the rippers." He turned his attention back to me. "And this is why I'm not destroying the contract."

"What does the contract have to do with anything?"

He shook his head and walked to the windows. A few rippers were hovering and he yanked the drapes shut. I didn't think it was for me, this time. I got the impression that the sight of them was making him more agitated right now.

A noise in the foyer heralded Burrom's arrival

and he strolled into the room without a care in the world, as if less than an hour ago we hadn't been stalked by crazy monsters.

He nodded to me and then looked at Cormac. "What did you want?"

I used to find it odd that this small Fae was the only one that would stand up to Cormac. I got it now.

"Why are you helping her? What are you getting in return?"

He looked to Cormac, then me, assessing the situation. "It's a private matter," Burrom said, puffing on the pipe he took everywhere with him.

Cormac left the room but returned in less than a minute with a sheet in his hand. "Maybe you need to look a little closer," he said and shoved the vellum paper at Burrom.

Burrom stood deathly still for a minute while he perused the paper, then shook his head while looking at me. "Why didn't you tell me you were joined with him?"

"Because I'm not, mostly. Or I don't consider..."

Burrom ignored my reply and turned back to Cormac. "It's already done. You need to honor it."

"Depends on what it is."

I'd never seen the small Fae so pissed off in the entire time I'd known him. He looked like he was going to burst a vein at any second. The look he threw at me said he would indeed try to eat me this very moment if he didn't need me.

"She's going to guard my burial ground."

Cormac stood back and nodded, seeming a bit placated by the answer. "Why didn't you ask me?"

"Because I don't even want you to know where it is. And I still don't want you to know." Burrom grumbled to himself, still agitated by the new turn of events. "Besides, what would you have asked for in return?"

"I would've worked with you," Cormac replied noncommittally.

Burrom snorted. "I know what your favors have cost me in the past."

Cormac relaxed his stance a bit and walked closer to me. "So what do you know? What happened today?" he asked Burrom.

"I can only speculate on my limited..."

"Tell me what you think. You made the deal. Honor it."

The little man walked further into the room, blustering the whole way about how Cormac shouldn't be getting involved. We both watched as he fussed about for a few minutes and then he finally sat on the couch and looked at us.

"I know how she was conceived. Her mother was barren. I think the senator used magic to jump start her. A magical in vitro, you could say. And not the weak magic, like Vitor has, but the strong stuff that comes from Earth, like I have."

"Why didn't you tell me this before?" I asked.

"You didn't ask," he explained. "I had no obligation to tell you my hypothesis."

I saw how this game was going to work. "Okay,

little man, I'm asking now. What else do you know or think? I want everything."

He pursed his lips and puffed on his pipe. I noticed he did that whenever he didn't want to talk.

"Burrom?"

"Fine. I think the rippers stayed away from you because of the amount of magic you have."

"Why?"

"Because, to them, it would be cannibalism."

"But why do they flock to me?" After everything that happened, it was pointless to deny it. I couldn't leave the drapes open without waking up to a slew of them.

"That I don't know."

Cormac stared him down this time.

"I really don't know." He waved his pipe in the air as he threw his hands up. "I think they find her to be an oddity. They recognize the magic she carries, even more so than mine, but their reaction is still strange," Burrom said.

"Can you help her?" Cormac asked.

"He tried to jump start me."

Burrom nodded, "I think it will help but we won't know for sure. It looks like it's going to take a while."

CHAPTER NINE

I made my way down to the conference room where we were meeting Oslo this morning. Our time was up. The plan was to send him back, agreeing to the truce, but without the insurance and let the chips fall where they may.

We all agreed, the senator was bluffing. He was afraid of an all-out war with us. If he could have killed me, he would have, but that didn't mean he couldn't inflict a whole ton of damage if he wanted.

I knew there was a problem as soon as I stepped into the hallway and saw Dodd and Buzz lingering outside the conference room door. Dodd looked like a can of gasoline with a lit fuse that was about to set him off. The moment his eyes met mine, and I saw the raw pain there, and I knew it was something to do with Sabrina.

"What's wrong?" I asked even though I was

scared to find out. I wanted to crawl back into bed, pull the covers over my face and pretend I was back in my trailer a year ago. But I couldn't do that. This was life, and when people looked upset, you asked what was wrong. The fact that lately, everyone was upset about something didn't seem to change the protocol. If things kept going the way they were, you had to wonder if at some point people would stop asking. Maybe, in a year or so, you'd only ask what was good when somebody looked happy.

"Oslo is gone and so is Sabrina and every other person on that list," Buzz explained. Dodd was too flustered to speak.

"Gone how?" It was a stupid question but sometimes when you are shocked, that's all you've got until the logical part of your brain starts back up.

"Gone! What do you mean how? We don't know," Dodd snapped and I let it go. I knew all about being snappy when you were stressed out. It was one of my specialties.

"We've got to get a group together and go after them." I looked at my funny phone's clock. "They can't have been gone that long. It's only eight a.m. they haven't had that much daylight yet."

"Cormac is going over the surveillance camera footage. If we can get a direction, it'll be easier," Dodd replied, finally finding his voice.

"I agree," Cormac said startling me as he

approached from behind.

"I'll go," I said. "And I'll ask Burrom." An awkward silence fell over the four of us as it was painfully obvious after last night, why I'd be the first to volunteer and want Burrom as well. We were the only confirmed people the rippers hadn't wanted to eat.

"Dodd, you stay behind and keep things under control here," Cormac said.

"No, not on this, Cormac. You can't ask me to stay behind this time. This means more to me than you."

"I don't think either of you should go," I said. They looked at me and continued on when neither of them liked what I said.

"Fine, but I want the group gathered and out within the hour. Everyone back before nightfall, whether you find them or not," Cormac said.

"Done," Dodd said. "I'm going to go gather supplies and volunteers. Meet me in the lobby in forty-five?" he asked, including me again now that my distasteful suggestion of him staying behind was off the table.

"Got it," I replied. I was going to head out and try to get Burrom on board when Cormac's hand on my arm stopped me. "I've got to go." The longer I have to negotiate with Burrom the better. He might want my first born, this time.

"Back by nightfall."

"I'll try."

"No, you'll do it."

"I'm not making any promises."

He pulled me into a windowless storage closet, stacked with shelves of paper and office supplies, across from the conference room.

He stood silent for a moment and that thing I couldn't put my finger on tugged at my brain. He seemed tenser than normal, even with the circumstances. "What's going on with you?"

He didn't answer but closed the distance between us, pressing me back against the shelves. His hands slid up my arms and over my shoulders until they cupped my head, tilting it back. He just stared down at me, not speaking.

"What?" I asked again, not understanding the volatility I felt in him.

"Nothing," he said.

His one hand moved from my hair, trailing along my jaw and down my neck. Then something snapped in his eyes and his mouth was on mine. His hands, so gentle before, roughly pulled me to him even more firmly.

His jaw moved along my neck and I felt the scruff of his face before he pulled back, then he was gone without another word.

CHAPTER TEN

I found Burrom on the seventh floor, surrounded by his brethren as they looked over a deck of cards spread out on the table.

"I need a minute," I said when Burrom looked up.

"Almost done."

The clock was ticking but I needed him happy, or in Burrom's case, not grumpy, so I tried to keep my patience. The man across from him laid out another card as I tried to figure out what kind of game they were playing. It was nothing I recognized from the casino and I clenched my teeth together trying to hold back my desire to scream that they needed to get a move on. I didn't have time for card games.

Burrom looked down at the last card turned over which was the Joker, then looked back to me. "I'm ready."

"You're ready?"

"Yes," he said, walking out of the room as I followed. "You wanted me to come, correct?"

"Did the uproar around the casino and me tracking you down in your suite give me away?"

He simply shrugged.

"Did you want to bring anything with you?"

"I need nothing." He looked to where I had a gun slung in a holster over my shoulder. "That's useless."

"Against rippers, yes. Against other things, maybe not."

"You wouldn't need it if you could simply channel your magic."

"Which I can't do yet."

"Because you are too in your head. You need to be of the universe to rule its powers."

"Okay, Yoda, but since I can't, let's try to think more practically." I was alongside him so he couldn't see me roll my eyes. I was getting so sick of everyone telling me what to do, how to do it and everything in between. "Why did you decide to come?"

"The cards told me it was the right choice. When I can't hear what the universe is saying, the cards tell me."

"Did the cards mention whether or not it was going to have a good outcome?"

"Yes, but only for me."

We entered the lobby where humans were clumped into groups of threes and fours. None of them said anything but their eyes spoke volumes as they surreptitiously glanced at me.

"Stop being silly," Burrom said to me.

"What are you talking about?"

"You didn't think they were going to throw you a party after you trashed the world, did you?"

"No, obviously not."

"You made a choice and you knew what might come of it. Don't be stupid about it now. You did what you thought was right. You had no way of knowing what closing the wormhole would do and if you hadn't, we wouldn't even be here. They just need to hate someone. Look, they hate me too. I don't go getting all mushy about it."

They probably did hate him. I didn't know if I liked him either. Difference was, I felt responsible, where he didn't seem to care one iota, just like Cormac. It made me wonder if I lived forever, if I'd be half dead inside too.

Dodd was waiting by the door with Dark and the resident wolf, Abby. Two more Keepers were also there, Donald and Alisa. Alisa didn't bother me but I hated Donald. Ever since the ride to NY, when he was laughing as the world was crumbling, he had rubbed me the wrong way.

Dodd's eyes shot over to Burrom for a second before coming back to me. "You ready?"

"We're here, aren't we?" Burrom answered the question for me.

"The footage showed Oslo, Sabrina and the others leaving and heading northeast on foot."

Dodd was checking the ammo he had packed while he talked. He'd need a lot if he planned on shooting the many guns strapped over his camo colored clothing.

"Let's get going then," I said, grabbing the backpack Dodd handed me.

He offered one to Burrom as well. Burrom took his, rifled through it and extracted a water canteen. He then shoved said canteen into my backpack. "Here," he said, as he shoved the backpack at a human passing by too close to avoid him.

"Happy Holidays," Burrom told him.

The human took it because I think he was too alarmed to *not* take it.

"Seriously, dude?" Dark asked of Burrom. "You could have at least said happy birthday. Then you would've had a shot of being correct. It's not even winter."

"I'm not a pack mule," Burrom replied, lifting his chin.

Dodd shook his head and the rest of us shrugged it off as we headed out the door.

I knew we could have taken a car for this, even though there wasn't a lot of gasoline available to waste. Gas was being reserved for supply scouting. At our current calculations, if the scouts didn't find more, we would be in total blackness sooner than I wanted to think about. Even still, the bigger issue was it would be easier to track them on foot. Tracking them by car would be nearly impossible.

As soon as we got a good fifty feet from the

casino, Dark let Abby off her lead. The leash was just for show inside the casino, so the humans didn't run screaming every time they saw her, and let her pick up the trail. From what I knew, Abby's sense of smell was comparative to Dark's in his wolf form. When Dark was in human form, Abby was stronger. I'd never seen Dark in wolf form but I'd seen others. Even if it was Dark, it was a scary scene to be sure.

"Did you see the footage? Did they look like they were somehow coerced?" I asked Dodd as we fell into a pace everyone was comfortable with, not too far behind Abby.

"It didn't look like it." There was disappointment in his voice and a wounded look in his eyes.

"You know, she did it for the good of the group."

"I know."

I grabbed his arm and held him back a minute.

"She did what she thought was right, just like you would've."

"We aren't together. She can do whatever she wants."

He pulled out of my grasp and walked back toward the group. He was too frustrated to see past his own feelings at that moment, so I let it go. I had my own conflicted emotions to sort through before I could fix anyone else.

Sabrina had been acting strangely, but I never thought she would do something like this. And how the hell did she get the rest of them on board? If I could've gotten my hands on Oslo right now, I would have broken the promise myself and wrung his neck.

Walking through the rubble, we all tried to stay toward the center of the road. Buildings were collapsing without notice all the time. There hadn't been a twister in this area in the last three days and the winds weren't bad today, but it didn't matter. Most of the structures were so impaired now, the smallest thing would bring them tumbling down.

As we followed Abby another mile, I realized this was the farthest I'd been from the casino since we'd returned. It burned the reality of the destruction into my brain. Bits of playing cards blew through the air and landed on the ground in front of me like a ticker tape parade, celebrating the end of the world. And this was the end. Maybe not of life, but most of the people living today would never see a normal city again in their lifetime.

My body followed the group even as my mind wandered in the surreal atmosphere. Every so often, I felt eyes peering at us, but whenever I turned, there was nothing. I knew there were still people out there that the rippers hadn't gotten to. I also suspected there were other creatures out there as well, things that might be worse than the rippers, but hadn't shown themselves yet.

The next movement that caught my eye wasn't

from ghosts lingering in burnt out buildings, it was from one of our own.

"Dark, are you okay?"

His hands were trembling and when he turned to me, a ravished look was in his eyes. Sweat was beaded on his forehead and he looked feverish.

"I can't hold it back any longer," he said.

"The change?"

He nodded. "It's the magic," he said through gritted teeth. Before he could explain any more, his clothes were shredding off his body. His jaw elongated, huge canine teeth growing. Blond fur grew and covered his now almost naked form. Muscles twitched and grew as his body shot up an additional two feet.

We all stopped and gawked. It was terrifying and mesmerizing. It was also something most of us hadn't seen happen in person. The wolves tended to transition in private. Now everyone knew why. Dark seemed completely vulnerable during the transition that took about five minutes. If there was an enemy around, five minutes of vulnerability was a lifetime.

"Dark, are you okay?" I asked after the change seemed to be slowing to an end.

"I don't think he can speak in this form," Dodd said.

Dark stiffly nodded his head in agreement, showing that he was coherent, if not quite comfortable yet. I trained my vision on his head, since he wore nothing but fur now and he had a surprisingly large appendage hanging below the waist. I knew it wasn't the polite thing to do, but I couldn't help and wonder if it was as large in his human form. Geez, Dark, I never would've guessed.

"Did you ever have this problem before? When things were normal?"

Dark shook his head in response.

"Do you want to continue?"

He nodded again.

"Okay, let's keep going then. We don't have a lot of time." What I wanted to say was *they* didn't have a lot of time. I'd keep going until the trail ran out, hopefully with Burrom, but alone if need be.

We started moving forward again, Abby still in the lead but now with Dark close behind her. I watched him, occasionally sniffing the air or along a wall that one of them must have touched as they passed.

When the sun was looming overhead at about one o'clock, I realized that some of our party would need to turn around or they wouldn't be able to make it back. We'd been walking this long and hadn't even made it to the desert yet.

"We need to stop." I swigged heavily from the water bottle stored in my pack and handed Burrom his, since he was too good to carry his own. I wished I were drinking something with more of a kick than water, but I couldn't risk dehydration, so I'd left my flask behind.

"What?" Dodd asked, clearly agitated.

"You've got to turn around." I wiped the sweat

off my forehead with my arm.

"Not happening, Jo." He shook his head and turned around and kept walking.

"If you don't turn around, you and the rest of the people here might not make it back. You could be eaten," I yelled after him.

Dodd stopped again and looked around, "Anyone want to go back, suit yourself. No hard feelings."

A deep rumbling sound emerged from Dark and he shook his massive head. Donald and Alisa both asserted they were staying as well, which I was a bit surprised by.

I turned to Burrom, who shrugged. "I might die but it won't be from rippers and it won't be now."

I looked at their faces and I didn't tell them what I was really thinking. I didn't want to watch them die all around me. I couldn't watch them die. I wanted to scream at them that I was at my breaking point. I couldn't take another thing. That if they wanted to die, couldn't they do it with someone else? These days, I was holding myself together with whiskey and denial. I didn't have my whiskey and denial was having a bad day.

I didn't say these things. I just started walking. At our current pace, we'd be in the middle of the Valley of Fire, a deserted part of the desert, come nightfall. Not a great place to try and find cover if we were attacked. Why oh why didn't I bring my flask?

We didn't stop for anything. We ate as we

walked. If someone had to go to the bathroom, they went and caught up quickly. We were all too aware of the ticking clock.

The crumpled buildings became more and more spread out until there was nothing but desert and the last rays of a fading safety were disappearing quickly.

I knew Cormac was probably going to be on a rampage back at the casino. He'd expect us to be walking in at any moment. That only added to the stress I already felt. I threw Burrom a look and slowed my pace. He did the same.

"If we get attacked, try to keep them in the center." I spoke low but I was pretty sure some of them heard me anyway.

He rolled his eyes at the imposition but I knew he'd do it.

And then we slowed to a stop. I saw Abby and Dark circling around. Shit. They'd lost the scent. Dark was still in werewolf form and he was pacing, unable to find their trail.

"This makes no sense. They didn't just disappear," Dodd said, following after Dark and visibly crowding him. "Dark, they've got to be here."

Dark whined a bit. Dark was Dodd's roommate and sidekick. He also worshipped the ground Dodd walked on. He wouldn't lose the trail if he could help it.

After another ten minutes of watching them try and fail, I was getting increasingly nervous.

Standing still like this made it much easier for the rippers to find us.

"We know where they were headed. We just keep going in that direction." At that very moment, I didn't care if we headed farther away from the casino or closer, anything but standing still.

"You're right," Dodd agreed. "We keep heading toward Arizona."

Back on the move again, I didn't feel relaxed but it was better than standing still.

About fifteen minutes later, both Dark and Abby started to pick up a trail again. Moving quickly, I followed as close as I could, hoping to be a living shield if the rippers came. I knew that I needed to be within a few feet if there was going to be any shot of it working. Donald and Alisa? They probably wouldn't fare too well and I'd have to increase my daily prescription of whiskey.

In the full dark, it was hard to see exactly where Dark and Abby were going, but I saw Dark suddenly kneel down next to a large boulder.

"What is it?" I asked, forgetting that Dark couldn't speak in this form.

I saw the feminine shape lying prone on the ground as I neared him. Her name was Colleen, the teenager with the purple eyes. She had been on the list of people the senator had demanded for insurance. This didn't bode well.

She was barely conscious when I kneeled down next to her.

"Colleen?" I asked and felt along her limbs for

injuries. There were several patches of wetness seeping through her shirt and she moaned when I touched her. I looked up at the others. "We've got to get her back to the casino. She's in bad shape."

"I can't stop. Sabrina's out there heading toward the senator," Dodd said.

"She's not."

Startled, we all looked down when we heard the soft voice of Colleen.

"Where are they?" I asked the girl, her eyes now partially open.

"We were attacked on our way there."

There was blood on her lips. This was bad, real bad.

"By who?" I asked.

"I don't know," she said. Her eyes drifted closed but I didn't think she was unconscious. Every word seemed like an effort to her.

"She is not going to make it very long if we don't get her help." I looked specifically toward Dodd now. "We all want to get Sabrina back and our only lead will die out here if we don't do something quick."

"Agreed," he said. "You take her back. I'm going to keep moving forward with Dark."

"Dodd, think for a second. I couldn't carry her back even if I agreed to that plan, and if we start splitting up, then we'll all be dead for sure." *You're dead,* is what I wanted to say, but I was trying to not enflame his ego along with his need to save his woman. "If she dies, we might not ever find

Sabrina. And if we don't get her help soon, she's dead." I whispered *she's dead,* hoping Colleen wouldn't hear me. I hoped Dodd was picking up on the general theme of what I was saying and I wouldn't have to scream *we're all going to die* over and over again.

"Okay," he said. "We turn around."

Dark made a growling noise and motioned his nose toward the helpless Colleen.

"Yes, I think that's a good idea," I replied and watched the eight foot tall werewolf scoop her up. He'd be able to carry her easier than anyone else in his wolf form.

Burrom dug his pipe out of his jeans pocket. "This isn't going how the cards said it would."

"What did the cards say?" I asked.

"You probably don't want to know," he replied as we walked in full darkness, Dodd flashing a light ahead of us.

"Tell me anyway," I said.

"Forget it. I spoke to soon."

I looked to where Burrom was staring up ahead. Dodd's flashlight caught a shimmer of their scaly skin as they made their way toward us. I couldn't tell how many there were, but the rippers had found us.

"You take the back," I said to Burrom as I quickly moved to the front.

"Now this is more of what I expected," I heard Burrom say as I ran to the front.

"Get behind me," I said to Dodd.

"Absolutely not," he replied. "No one dies for me."

"I. Won't. Die." I stressed each word. "*You* will."

He took precious seconds that we didn't have but finally relented. "Valid point," he replied and then allowed me to step in front of him.

With everyone behind me, I could concentrate solely on what was coming at us. As the rippers got closer, I saw there were fifteen of them.

They made strange clicking and hissing noises as they edged closer. I didn't remember that noise from last time and I'm sure I would have. It filled the air with a foreboding and I had a really bad hunch it meant they were preparing to feed.

They stopped three feet away from me, which was way too close for comfort. They started to fan out and circle around us.

"Burrom," I called, not wanting to turn my back on the rippers.

"They're closing in," he yelled from behind me, voice raised but calm.

It was a lot easier to be calm when you knew you weren't going to be dinner and you didn't care if the people around you were possibly dessert.

I waited...no, hoped the silver smoke would appear and save my ass once again. Was it somehow now a part of me? And if it was, why couldn't I use it? The stuff that seeped out of me hadn't been useful at all.

The rippers' eyes were darting back and forth

between where Dodd stood and the other Keepers. They weren't paying attention to me at all, tonight. They were hungry and only had eyes for their next meal.

They were also nearly opaque now. My hunch was that a diet of human meat was what brought them fully into this new existence, and they'd had plenty of it. God only knew how many lives had been sacrificed to them.

They edged in closer and closer, their attention remaining on the Keepers of the group.

"Dark," I said.

He growled in reply, but I knew the anger in it was directed solely for the rippers.

"Form a triangle with me and Burrom."

We readjusted with the Keepers in the center but it wasn't going to be enough. They maintained a larger distance from me than Burrom or Dark. The horrible clicking noises they were making intensified, as they seemed to be becoming more excited at the prospective kill to come.

Donald and Dodd released a spray of bullets into the group of rippers but they simply bounced off their tough skin.

Finally, after several tense moments, one of them made a lunge for Dodd. He parried and slit a gash into its arm. It recoiled back with a screech, but another one simply took its place.

Fear and anger boiled up inside of me as I saw them lunge again for Dodd. "Get away from him!" I screamed. Silver mist leaked out of my mouth as I yelled. The ripper looked like it was being physically pushed away from Dodd.

"Keep going," Burrom said.

"Get back," I said, and again, the silver mist flowed from me. The rippers moved back a little further. Their attention was fully on me now and their clicking and hissing stopped. "Come on, let's start moving forward."

"Are you sure?" Alisa asked, terror tingeing her words.

"I don't know how I'm doing this or how long it's going to work for." I couldn't stop and argue with them. I needed to get them moving and now. "I'm moving forward. You either move with me or you can stay here to die." It was a bluff that I hoped they'd fall for.

I took a step forward and everyone moved with me. It had taken us nine hours to get here. The walk back was going to be pure torture if the rippers stayed with us the entire time.

"Dark, how's Colleen?" I asked, trying to calculate how long we had and if we'd make it back in time to save her with the much slower pace.

He replied with a high-pitched howl that I interpreted to mean not so good.

I didn't want the young girl to die but knowing she was the only lead to someone I cared for made it that much worse.

"Dark, could you travel faster without us?"

"He nodded," Burrom said.

"A lot faster?"

"Yes," Burrom spoke again for Dark.

"I don't think they like your wolf form. Give Colleen to Dodd for a minute and step away from the group." I tried to think back to the wolves that had been killed. Was it just Dark or was it the wolf form? I knew I was asking a lot of him, but we'd never get Colleen back alive at this pace.

Dark moved to the front next to me and then ahead. The rippers didn't bother with him at all. He circled and loped back to my side.

"Dark, take Colleen and try to get her back as quick as you can. We'll follow behind you."

Dark let out another growl. I didn't need this one interpreted for me. "I'll get them back. I got this. You need to get her back because if she's still bleeding out, she'll be dead soon."

I chanced looking back for a moment and letting the rippers out of my sight, in favor of checking on Colleen. Her head lay limp over Dodd's arm, her small form lifeless. Blood was dripping down Dodd's shirt and staining it.

Dark gently lifted Colleen from Dodd's arms with his large clawed hands and returned back to me.

"You've got to get her back as quick as you can."

He leaned his muzzle down to her, sniffing along her neck. He looked back to me and nodded.

A second later, he broke out of the group in a fast gait. I held my breath as he shot straight into the rippers but they paid him almost no mind as he zigzagged between them, heading back toward the casino.

Once he was gone, Burrom fell into place holding up the rear again. The rippers kept pace with us as we went. Whenever the rippers started to edge in, I spoke and they stepped back.

We'd barely started back and I was already exhausted. However this magic worked, it wasn't easy. It was draining me more by the second, each word costing me more than the last. This was going to be one long walk back.

CHAPTER ELEVEN

"Did Dark make it back with Colleen?" I asked Buzz the minute we walked into the Lacard lobby at three in the morning. The place was quiet as we stepped inside. The rippers had followed us all the way back and increased in number as we moved, most of them more interested in staring at me than anyone else. I'd repeatedly told them to leave but was too exhausted by the end. For the last quarter of the trip, we'd kept everyone sandwiched between Burrom and me. Only a handful still lingered in the distance as we went inside the casino.

Buzz's blue eyes widened and his eyebrows rose. "Cormac's *pissed*."

"I'll deal with him later. Did Dark make it back with the girl?"

"Yes."

"Is she..."

"Alive."

"Who's taking care of her?" After Dark left, I had nothing but time to think of all the worst case scenarios. Sabrina was gone and I wasn't sure there was another doctor in the casino that could help her.

"One of Burrom's people."

I nodded, leaving him immediately for the seventh floor. I didn't realize Burrom and Dodd were behind me until I got into the elevator, not having the energy for the stairs. I stepped in and hoped the gas supply was running strong. Dodd looked visibly agitated and Burrom was just too scary to be stuck in the close confines of an elevator with for more than a minute or so.

"Unit #711," Burrom's guy told us as soon as we stepped off the elevator, knowing instinctively what we wanted to know.

Cormac was standing by the girl's bedside when we entered the room, talking to a young woman who seemed to be checking on Colleen. Our eyes met and their intensity made me shiver. Again, the thought that something more was going on with Cormac than I knew sprang to mind but I was prioritizing issues right now. Hunches were low man on the totem pole.

I stepped up alongside the bed next to him.

His face told me he had questions even before he spoke. "Don't disappear."

I nodded. "How's she doing?"

"There is a lot of bruising and internal damage," the young woman said. I knew she was Fae so I guessed she was older than the twenty or so years she appeared.

"You're a doctor?"

"Yes, but not normally to humans." It wasn't said with rancor but insecurity. "There were a couple of puncture wounds," she pointed to several places on Colleen's torso, "but I believe I have her stabilized."

"Did you have to operate on her?"

"Cut her open? I don't do that sort of thing." The doctor put her hands up as if to ward off such a ghastly suggestion.

"Then what are you doing?" The image of her chanting over Colleen's bedside didn't instill much confidence in me.

"I've treated her like I would any magical creature." The nurse pulled Colleen's shirt up slightly and showed me a gaping wound coated with a black tar like substance.

"Will that work on a human?" I asked.

"I don't know about normal humans, but I don't believe that's what she is any longer."

"She's not human?" Cormac asked.

"She's one of the *changed* now, they are no longer human the way you would think of them."

I looked down at the young teen and didn't see what she meant. "Other than her eyes, she looks human to me."

"Have either of you touched her?" the doctor

asked and we both shook our heads. "Feel her," the doctor encouraged.

I reached down and took the girl's hand. She was a bit cool, probably due to her currently bad circulation, but she felt normal. I shrugged and looked at the Fae doctor.

"No, don't just touch her; feel her like you would a wormhole or whatever it is you people do."

I knew that for creatures who were used to dealing with magic their whole lives, these extra senses were like seeing and smelling but I still consciously had to think of it.

The second I did, I felt a jolt of energy pass through her skin and I dropped her hand instinctively.

"You'll get used to it," the Fae doctor said.

I nodded, it hadn't been painful, just unexpected.

"I've done everything I can, or know how to do," the doctor said. "Now we just wait."

"I'll stay with her," I said to the doctor. "I'm sure you're exhausted." *And you're a little creepy.*

Cormac put a hand on my back. "We've got other issues to handle. I'll send some people to help her."

"I'll have my people do it," Burrom said from the door, eyeing Colleen in a way that set off a couple of alarms in me. I'd forgotten he and Dodd were in the room.

"We'll alternate shifts," Cormac replied.

I suspected neither Burrom nor Cormac were doing this for completely altruistic reasons. Cormac, Dodd and I wanted the information only she had. I didn't know what Burrom's motives were, other than he liked knowledge and here was the perfect opportunity to acquire a guinea pig. After all, knowledge is power.

And as for power, what was happening to her? To all of us, for that matter. "Where's Dark?" I asked Cormac, thinking of how he'd lost control of his form for the first time ever since I'd known him.

"At Dodd's, trying to change back. He scared the hell out of the humans when he got in."

It had probably been quite a sight, a hairy eight feet tall monster carrying a young girl dripping blood.

"Somebody needs to check on him," I said.

"I'll do it," Dodd replied and left the room.

"Keep me posted," Cormac told the Fae doctor and then steered me out in front of him.

He followed me as I headed to the stairwell.

"The scouting group found a large stash of gas today. It's safe to use the elevator."

I kept walking in the same direction. "Nope. I'd rather use the stairs."

"Have you always been this crazy? I used to think it was just you needing to transition, but I'm starting to have my doubts."

"What's crazy about not using the elevator?"

"You were afraid to go outside but then you stalked Tracker, who was an obvious threat, who you knew could kill you. You stay out all night with the rippers but then you won't use the elevator. You don't see something off about those things?" His voice echoed up and down the stairwell but we were the only ones in there.

"When I didn't outside for a while because I was afraid of flying away, it didn't cause harm to anyone, while Tracker did. The rippers could've killed Dodd and the other Keepers, while taking the stairs all the time just gives me exercise. How do you *not* see the logic of my choices?"

I pushed open the door to the penthouse. If someone asked when it had become home, I couldn't have told them, but I knew with perfect clarity that it was indeed home. The night of New York, when the shit hit the fan and the world was torn apart, it was where I wanted to be most. When everything was falling to pieces around me, I'd known with absolute clarity where I wanted to be.

"Okay, let's have it," I said, knowing he was going to haunt me until he had his say. I stepped into the beige oasis, also known as the living room. Nothing about me was beige. I wondered if he'd let me redecorate the place now that everyone knew he wasn't beige either.

"You were supposed to be back by dark. You don't know for certain that the rippers won't eat you."

"I do now." I collapsed onto the couch and kicked my feet up. He was stalking around the room. Cormac was a machine these days, never resting. How was he doing it? I was operating on little to no sleep and it was obvious in my every move. But he never looked tired.

"Why? What happened?" he asked.

I told him about how the mist seeped out and the rippers had been forced back just by my voice alone.

"But you still haven't seen it?"

"Like I used to? No. Not since New York." I didn't add that I wondered if somehow on that night I had absorbed it into myself. That the silver strands were now part of me, maybe always had been.

I looked at Cormac, wondering if he was thinking the same thing but his face was unreadable again. Then he left the room and I relaxed deeper into the couch cushions. That had been pretty easy. I'd been expecting a much larger fight than that.

I just lay there and stared through the windows, too tired to stand anymore. An occasional ripper passed by, glancing in out of curiosity, but I was becoming adjusted to them and just changed my view to the other side of the window and tried to remember what the glittering view used to look like, even at the wee hours of the morning like now.

Cormac walked back in and I rolled my eyes. I'd relaxed too soon.

"Hold out your hand," he said as he stopped

next to me.

I did as he asked but immediately dropped the black-shrunken piece of flesh to the ground.

"Ugh, what is that!" I looked at it there, lying on the floor.

"That was the contract between us." He stood a few feet away from me, just staring.

I looked back, trying to gauge his mood. Nothing. "It's completely destroyed? That easily?" I didn't think he would do it. He actually did it. Now that it was gone, I didn't know how I felt.

"It wasn't that easy, but I created it. It wasn't triggered, so I could destroy it."

"So that's it. It's just handled. We're unengaged or whatever?" The thing looked like it had been charred but there were no ashes in my hand. It was over. I was free, so why wasn't I as relieved as I thought I'd be?

"Yes," he said. "Are you happy now?"

Did he want me to be happy or was I supposed to be nonchalant? I watched him standing there, not moving an inch. I hated when he shut me out like this and I had no idea what he was thinking. If I'd done something someone asked me to do, I'd be thankful. I'd been asking him to get rid of it, so maybe I was supposed to be happy.

"Yes, thank you. It will just make everything much easier now, I think." The black flesh lying there kept drawing my gaze.

He didn't say a word in reply and I started to ramble on.

"I didn't think you'd do it, but it's for the best. I'm way too young to be married after all, and this way we can just take our time and see if it's the right thing." I didn't know if I was convincing him or myself anymore. "Really, this was the right thing." I tore my eyes off the dead contract and looked up at Cormac and a knot formed in my stomach.

His face wasn't emotionless anymore, but cold.

"You once told me you were broken. I didn't believe you, at first. Actually, that's not true, I knew you were broken but I thought I could fix you." He took a couple steps away from me and I couldn't take my eyes off of him as my insides clenched and I realized belatedly that he hadn't wanted me to be happy.

He turned back to me, now almost across the room. He was distancing himself from me.

"Even after I started to doubt whether I could make you want me the way I wanted you, I decided it didn't matter. I'd take you broken, if that was the only way I could have you."

I started to relax just a hair. This would be okay.

"But then, at every turn, you cut me off."

"I just need time," I said.

"No, you don't. Or you shouldn't. When you care for someone, you don't want to waste time."

"But I'm younger than you, it's different."

"You're old enough. If time were the problem, I could wait forever. But it's not."

"I don't understand why you are acting like

this. So, now what? I marry you or you're done with me?"

"No, we're just done." He turned and walked toward his room. He didn't bother to look at me as he uttered his final words. "I'll arrange for you to get a room on Dodd's floor."

Why was he doing this? I didn't call after him. I didn't get up and pack my things. I just sat there, frozen, as the last certain thing in my life was ripped from my grasp.

Cormac was done with me?

CHAPTER TWELVE

"She's awake and speaking," Dark said as he burst into the penthouse living room at nine the next morning. I was having coffee and nursing my horrible evening hangover, this one having nothing to do with booze, as I wondered how many more mornings I'd have before I was booted. Had Cormac really been serious or was this just a bully tactic he was using on me? My emotions felt like raw skin that was sensitive to the slightest touch.

"Huh?" I asked.

"Colleen, she's awake."

I splashed my coffee on myself in my rush to stand and get moving. Dark waited for me by the door.

"Did she say anything?" I asked as we both got into the elevator. I hated the elevator but I wanted to get to Colleen as quickly as possible.

"She just woke."

"Are you okay?" I asked, since we had maybe a whole minute of downtime waiting for the elevator to get to the seventh floor. This was the first time I'd seen him since we'd both gotten back.

"A little sore, no biggy. When the change is forced, it makes the muscles hurt." He cracked his neck as he spoke.

"What exactly happened?"

"I've been feeling it just beneath the surface since New York. Stress can force the change. I should've been able to keep control of it, even with the additional strain, but there's something about this new world that's making it harder."

"Everything is harder these days," I said, as I looked at him in his t-shirt and ripped jeans. He looked like a carefree young guy if you didn't look closely, or didn't know him well. But the strain was there, in the down turned corners of his mouth and the weariness of his eyes.

"I know it's screwing with you, too." He smiled then, but it was the smile of co-commiseration, with no real happiness behind it. "Besides, the human vaporizer trick, I hear you've got a bit of a drinking problem these days."

"I don't have a drinking problem. I've got a shitty life problem and I'm self medicating because we've lost our only real doctor and we're out of antidepressants."

"We've all got shitty lives," Dark said. "My life sucks, too."

I grabbed his arm and turned him to face me

so I could make sure he understood my next words. "Dark, I destroyed the world as we know it."

It took him a second but then he shrugged in acceptance. "Dodd's got a couple of extra bottles of whiskey, if you're running low."

"Thank you. I appreciate the support."

The doors slid open just in time for me to stop dwelling on the complete mess everything was. I stepped out into the hallway and remembered exactly where I needed to go. When I got to the room, the Fae doctor was already there and so was Cormac. Burrom was standing back along the wall.

Looking at Cormac, I searched for some sign that last night had just been one of our tiffs, and he hadn't been serious. He didn't even look at me. When he did look up, his gaze passed over me as if I weren't there. I looked down at Colleen, to avoid staring at him.

"She doesn't look awake," I said, watching the girl lie lifeless on the bed. The moment I spoke the words, her purple eyes fluttered open.

I leaned down next to her and took her hand. "Colleen?"

She pulled her hand back, looking wary, and I let it go. "Does anyone know if she has any family?" I asked.

"No," Colleen answered for herself and I watched as she tried to pull herself into a sitting position. I wanted to help but I was afraid to touch her again. The way she was eyeing up Cormac was probably the reason he wasn't approaching her either.

Dark took the initiative and stepped around me to help her. She didn't look very comfortable with him either, but she didn't pull back.

"What happened?" Cormac asked and I could see the girl's eyes open just a hair bigger. "Colleen, you need to tell us," he continued. I watched as he started to lean forward over the bed.

The girl's eyes darted to Dark and then shifted back to Cormac.

Bullying was just going to shut this girl down, but I found I was somewhat afraid to speak to Cormac. I didn't know if I could handle him outright ignoring me in front of everyone. "Cormac, I need you to check on something with me. She's okay. Let's give her some space."

Our eyes truly met for the first time. I held my breath as he hesitated. He might really be done with me and it made my head spin. Finally, after a couple of tense moments, he nodded and followed me out of the room, throwing a last glance at Dark that told him he better get the desired information.

"She would've talked," he said once we were a healthy distance away down the hall.

"I'm not doubting your ability to intimidate, but wouldn't it be nice if we got the information without traumatizing the girl further?"

"Only if it doesn't take too long." He still wasn't looking at me when he spoke, but walking down the hall.

"Where are you going?" I asked.

"To check on the field."

I followed him down the stairs to the main floor, not speaking. We walked through what used to be the casino floor that had recently developed makeshift divides. There were Fae selling magical charms in one corner and humans selling goods they had scavenged in another. Werewolves were lingering here and there. I'd heard a rumor they were offering protection in return for food and other items, but I hadn't had it confirmed. Right now, it was still just an unsettling rumor.

Stares fleetingly landed on me as we passed through but moved quickly on to a different subject with Cormac by my side.

Cormac was a whole other type of problem. I'd never had someone accept me so fully, who made me feel safe even in chaos and then hurt me so badly. It felt like my soul was being ripped into little pieces. I wanted him, but I was having a hard time resigning myself to what he'd done, what he would still be willing to do. And now, I didn't have words for what it felt like to know he could just cut me out of his world like this. Had I ever even really meant anything to him? If I did, how could he be acting this coldly toward me?

I followed him outside and around the side of the building to the larger area. The cement had been torn up and sod was being laid down in its place. It had probably been torn up from the front yards of houses that no longer had residents. A small doll was lying in the heap of grass they hadn't gotten to yet. I hoped it was hastily abandoned on their way to a safer place and not the bleak alternative.

"It's not a huge area but I figured I'd send the next scouts out to see if they could round up some chickens. If a storm comes in, they're building a ramp over there that leads into the casino and will shelter them from the storm."

"How did you get so many people to help?" I asked looking at the twenty or so men laying the recycled grass.

"They liked it better than the work detail they currently have."

He's showing me what he's up to. Maybe he wasn't done. Maybe I just had to throw him a bone?

"Thanks for showing me," I said, smiling as sweetly as I could.

"We had a couple of minutes to kill." His face was stone.

Cormac's phone lit up and he answered it quickly. "Okay," he replied briefly into the phone and hung up. "Dark's got our answers."

I watched him walk back toward the casino, leaving me to follow...or not. I did, but I wasn't following him, I told myself. What was the point? He was really done. The guy had shot me, bullied me and was an all-around ass, sometimes. I wasn't going to be some idiot with Stockholm syndrome. If he couldn't take it slow, then I didn't want him either.

CHAPTER THIRTEEN

"She didn't want to admit that she was different, one of the *changed,*" Dark told the two of us as we sat on the couch back in the penthouse.

"Did you tell her the purple eyes were a dead giveaway?" Cormac said.

First he kicks me out and now he's stealing my lines?

"I didn't know this, but the humans have been getting aggressive toward the *changed,*" Dark continued.

I looked down. If I hadn't been such a wimp I might have known, but I'd been avoiding the humans. I walked through their areas but not among them. I'd stopped trying to talk to them.

"Does she know where they went?" I asked just as Dodd burst into the room.

"What did you get?" Dodd asked. "Do you

know where Sabrina is?"

"Let me just explain this from the beginning. Sabrina had contacted the other people on the list, who were all *changed*. She explained the situation to them. There was no coercion at all, she simply told them what was at stake and what was being requested by the senator. They agreed to think about it, meet the next day and make a group decision.

"The humans have been getting a bit unfriendly toward the *changed* and lumping them in with anything not human. They were getting some of the blowback directed toward us, who they view as the cause of all this. That being said, we can all understand the additional motivation to leave.

"They all met and decided to go. Sabrina spoke to Oslo to coordinate the logistics, because she knew you wouldn't agree to this," Dark looked at Cormac. "Or you," he added, looking at Dodd. "It gets interesting here. They were all afraid to leave at night but Oslo informed them that the rippers weren't a threat to the *changed*. They only feed on non-magical beings."

It was just like Burrom had thought, but it still didn't completely fit. "What about the Keepers that were eaten that first evening?" I asked. "That doesn't make sense."

"I asked Colleen, but she didn't know enough about that to question what she was being told."

I didn't doubt it. The humans hadn't been

included in a lot of the meetings and no one wanted to talk about that night. Only one issue remained. "Sabrina knew. Why would she not question it?"

"I have no answer for that," Dark said. "Maybe she did but Colleen doesn’t know."

"So what happened between then and when we found her?" Dodd said, not caring about anything else.

"They left at three in the morning, with Oslo leading the way. They made it to Fire Valley, where they were attacked by a group of humans that were also *changed*. Colleen didn't know how many. It was dark and they'd been avoiding using any lights."

"How did she know they were *changed*?" Dodd asked in full interrogation mode.

"One of them had wings and another breathed fire."

"Yeah, that would do it," I said.

"She said in the chaos, she didn't see everything that went down. The *changed* with the wings was the one that tried to take her. His fingers grew talons when she tried to get away. Then, while she was struggling, a bolt of lightning came out of nowhere and hit him. When it hit him, his talons clenched and dug into her, causing the puncture wounds she has.

"She thinks she did it somehow, because he was holding her when it happened and she wasn't affected by it."

"So where was this creature then? He didn't die?" Dodd asked.

"She heard who she thought was the leader scream to leave her behind. They grabbed their wounded guy and left."

"Does she know where they went?" Dodd pressed.

"No, only has a vague direction."

Dodd, who'd been pacing the room, slammed his fist down on the bar.

"This isn't bad. Now we know where to start and we also know who to send," Cormac said. "I want an examination of every person here. We need an exact count of the *changed*."

"We can't force them to come," I said preemptively.

The look on his face said otherwise. "I feed and shelter them. I can do whatever I please." He ignored the look on my face and looked back at the guys. "Dark, start seeing what you can dig up."

Dark got up to leave and Dodd went with him. No one had time to sit around these days, with the way things were going.

"Dodd, I need a minute before you go back," Cormac said, halting him before he left.

"Sure, what's up?"

Cormac looked at me and I instantly knew what this was about. He was waiting for me to tell Dodd I needed a room on his floor. He was letting me ask, to save face. He didn't seem to care it was going to crush me to do it. Did he think I could turn to stone, like he had?

I looked at Cormac. Nothing. Not a glimmer of regret. Not a glimmer of anything for that matter.

I cleared my throat. "I'm going to need another room."

Dodd's jaw dropped as his eyes shot from mine to Cormacs.

I cleared my throat before I continued. "Cormac thought your floor would be a good idea, but I've got another arrangement in mind."

It took Dodd a second to speak. "Okay, just let me know." He hightailed it out of the room quicker than I'd ever seen.

"Where are you going?" Cormac asked, the second Dodd shut the door.

"Not your problem," I said, rage starting to replace the hurt I was feeling. I left him standing there to go pack my bags. I wouldn't spend another night in this penthouse. I wish I could say the same thing about the whole casino, but there wasn't much help for that yet. Maybe after we found Sabrina.

CHAPTER FOURTEEN

Cormac asked all human refugees to report to the seventh floor where Burrom and his people would check for an *unusual* amount of magic. Not just magic, but unusual amounts. Some humans had a certain small amount of magic naturally, even in normal times. They would be called psychics, seers, freak shows, or maybe just weird Aunt Sally. The guess was that it was mostly these humans that were now the *changed*.

Not a single person showed up. From the way I heard they'd been treated lately, I didn't blame them one iota. It was supposed to be confidential, but when a floor full of people saw you get branded as *magical*, there was no way it was staying secret.

Next, Cormac demanded it. He sent Burrom and his not so merry crew out amongst them, to document every human with an abnormal amount of magic. It was no secret why Burrom had agreed to help. He was as crafty as they came, always keeping his options open, looking at every angle. And the one thing I've learned about Burrom was he liked power, not because he wanted to take over, but because he was old and smart and knew how to survive. I understood why he was one of the few people on a very short list of those Cormac respected, even if he didn't exactly like him.

I wasn't sure about trusting Burrom myself, after the other night's debacle. I was running at a deficit in the trust department, which was why on Monday morning, I was following him around from human to human. One thing I already knew for sure, being part of the magical Gestapo wasn't doing a lot for my current social standing, especially since everyone seemed to already know I'd moved onto Burrom's floor.

I'd shown up there yesterday with a hastily packed bag like a beggar. I knew he'd take me in and I knew it was one of the last places Cormac would want me to go. Too bad for him. You don't get to kick someone out and then dictate where they move; even Cormac couldn't pull that off. Well, he might be able to with most people, but I wasn't going to let him.

My room was a bit of a shock to me. It was the only room Burrom had open and it looked like it had been done over with a medieval castle in mind. Burrom tried to tell me it had spontaneously looked like that one day, which was why no one wanted it. My guess was someone who was good at charms was having a little fun with the casino decor.

Walking down the hallway with him now, I spotted another patch of stone. Patch might be downplaying a spot that reached from floor to ceiling, six feet wide.

"Burrom, you've to get your people to stop doing this," I said as my hand ran over stone that felt alarmingly real to the touch.

"Not my people."

"Who's doing it then?"

"Not sure, and don't care. I'm more concerned that you don't trust me, Jo," Burrom said as we worked through the room check. "It hurts me, Jo, that you would think so little of me. I thought when you decided to move in we were forming a real bond."

I almost snorted at his comment. Burrom was as thick skinned as they came. Nothing hurt his feelings and my lack of trust for him was becoming one of his favorite jokes. "Am I wrong?"

"I didn't say that," he replied with his own chuckle as we hung back and waited for the female Fae with us to knock on the door of the ninth floor and ask for admittance.

The people inside didn't answer but we knew they were in there. The female Fae, Angela, read them the same warning we had been giving out since we began. "If you don't open up, this room will have the locks changed by this evening and you will be forced to find new lodgings outside of the casino."

We waited the five minutes it took most of them to open. Earlier in the day, one group made us wait fifteen minutes. At sixteen minutes, Burrom had scared them with some crazy Fae mojo that made them think the room was on fire. They'd run right out. The other humans must have been listening at the doors or something. The rest of that floor was a breeze after that.

The door finally creaked open to reveal what appeared to be a young husband and wife, with what might once have been a human toddler. It was hard to tell, with the black fur and the hissing, if a child was indeed still under there.

We strolled in and another of the Fae with us laid a hand upon the husband, single shake of his head. Wife was next up, and again, single shake of his head. When he went to lay a hand upon the cat child, the mother clung tightly to her. I wasn't sure why we even bothered to confirm. The yellow eyes and fangs weren't enough?

And holy cow, how many more *changed* like this were hiding in their rooms?

"How long has she been like this?" I asked the mother.

"It started slowly, with just some little areas of peach fuzz, but then we woke up one day and she was like this. Are you going to take her? She's only two years old." Tears streamed down the mother's face and the father positioned himself in between us, like he'd have a chance to stop us if we decided to take her.

"No one is going to take your child," I said before Burrom or any of the other Fae could speak.

The mother's eyes came to rest upon me. "You swear?"

I couldn't swear for everyone so I made the only promise I could. "They'd have to do it over my dead body." I'd kill Cormac myself if he tried. I glanced over at Burrom and he looked everywhere but me. I didn't add that it could possibly come to that and then they were on their own.

We left the room and the family with a false sense of peace. Burrom took the accounting sheet from our Fae helpers as we both headed to our next potential victims -- oops, I mean humans.

"Don't touch her, Burrom," I said, referring to the cat girl.

"She's a babe. I'd have no use for her."

"And when she's not?"

"I'm going to ground before that will happen."

I nodded. I could accept that. I wasn't sure when exactly he was going to ground, but he'd be there long after she became an adult. At that point, she was on her own. Kids, yeah, okay, I'd go down with the ship for them. In this world, as an adult, you had to help yourself a little, because there wasn't any hero showing up to save you.

At some point, I'd thought I was a hero in the making. All I made was a gigantic mess. My cape had gone up in flames that night in New York. The small fragment of the human population left hated me. I'd grown up a loner, only watching out for myself. Then at some point, I'd started to care. I'd started to want people. Now look at me. What a mess. I longed for the days I didn't care. And to make matters worse, I'd emptied the last contents of my flask a floor ago.

It took the entire day to go through all the floors and we still missed the lion's share. Word was spreading fast and people were disappearing. I didn't know where they hid, but as word got out, less and less people were in their rooms by the end of the day.

I'd still seen more than I wanted to. There was a spider woman on floor fifteen that had a cocoon built in the corner of the room. On eighteen, we had a giant. The guy used to be a professional linebacker, but now he couldn't sit in a chair without crushing it. A woman on twenty couldn't leave the shower stall for more than hour because of the water that streamed from her pores and there was a human pretzel on thirty-two. Today had been a serious revelation.

When I got to the penthouse, I immediately went to the bar. I knew what had to be done next and I was going to need a little anesthetic to go through with it. I also needed something to take the edge off seeing Cormac.

Burrom sat down and laid the list on the table as we waited for the rest of the crew to show. This was a "closed-door" meeting. I poured myself another finger of whiskey. Nothing good ever came of these, and this time I'd be holding a gun on the virtual firing squad.

I looked down at my glass and added another finger of the amber liquid. It wouldn't make it right, but it would make it a lot easier to be wrong.

Would I be able to live with myself if I went even further down this path? The thought scared me. I swallowed back the drink before I asked myself any more questions I'd prefer not to know the answer to. I was officially living through the apocalypse; this wasn't the right time for moral dilemmas or deep soul searching.

Cormac and Dodd walked in next, followed by Rogo and Vitor a few minutes later, which made Sabrina's absence that more obvious. I missed having at least a little estrogen in the room besides myself.

Cormac silently pointed at the list on the table. Burrom nodded and I watched as Cormac reached down and started flipping through.

"Everyone under eighteen is on a different sheet," I said, still feeling the burn of the liquor in my throat. That had been my personal contribution to saving the young'uns. I hoped he got the hint and would leave them alone.

He nodded, not bothering to look up from the pages. Any chance of this being civil between us disappeared as quickly as my next shot.

"The *changed* are about ten percent of the

human population," Burrom said.

"Looks closer to twelve," Cormac corrected, still looking through the list. "This should be enough to do everything."

"Everything" entailed a food detail, a gas detail and a Sabrina detail, all forced labor that would be immune to the rippers. How did it come to this? Do what we want or you and your families get booted out. No one had spoken the words, but we'd all known what was coming as soon as the idea of a list had been formulated.

It made me wonder how close to the door I was now that Cormac wasn't interested anymore. Nah, considering the contempt he was barely hiding now, I'd already be out if that was going to happen. But the humans, that was a different story altogether.

If we didn't force the *changed* to help, would we survive? If they wanted to stay, they should have to kick in, right? But sending someone out there when we weren't even sure of what really kept the rippers at bay? Not to mention, we didn't know what else may lie in wait, or when another freak storm would spring up.

Cormac finally looked up from the papers.

"We've got enough here to replace the people we've lost for the food squads and fuel squads. These numbers are much better than I anticipated." He looked to me and then Burrom. "And these all had magic levels high enough to probably make it through a night?"

Probably? Was I the only one that found that disturbing? I looked around the room and I knew I was.

"Yes," Burrom said.

I was feeling all warm and fuzzy from the booze and yet I still cared. "Fuck it," I said and took a swig right from the bottle.

Cormac turned toward me and squinted his eyes just slightly.

"That's not your normal brand," he said in an unflattering way. "I guess these days you'll drink anything, if it comes in the form of a shot."

"Trust me. You all want me drunk for this." I lifted the bottle in a silent cheers salute to him and the room.

He turned back to the rest of the group. No one else looked or said a word, maybe preferring to pretend that I wasn't getting drunk in the corner by myself.

Cormac took another quick glance in my direction, or more accurately, at the bottle I held. I lifted it to my lips and took a swig, egging him on.

He turned away, not taking the bait. "Let's vote," he said.

Everyone in the room had to vote. It was a complete sham, since the only person whose opinion mattered was Cormac's. Still, they continued on like it counted.

Burrom said yes, no shock there.

"This will cut down on the runs my people take? I don't want more than one of my guys out there per squad," Rogo said.

"Done," Cormac replied.

"Fine by me." It was another typical vote. Rogo didn't care a wink about the humans. He just wanted to secure a better deal for himself.

"And you promised me humans for Sabrina," Dodd chimed in next, all too eager to get his hands on some human resources.

"Yes, I told you that is a priority."

Dodd nodded, at least having the decency to look a little ashamed.

Vitor didn't argue for anything, just said yes. Of all the people in the room, I found myself feeling for Vitor the most. He was as out of place as Ashley was in the second half of Gone with the Wind. Just a shell of the man he used to be. I didn't know if it was losing his sister or the world the way it was. The ones that had less fight inside to begin with were faring the worst, if they remained alive. I mean, hell, I wasn't jumping out of bed in the mornings either, these days. When it came down to it, we'd all been slowly losing something inside. For some, they slowly lost the drive to fight for survival. For others, that fight was so strong it drove out the last shreds of their humanity.

It was there now, as they all turned their stares towards me. Colder. Meaner. Desperate. And then I realized, I could drink that whole bottle, it wouldn't change anything. I couldn't vote yes on this. I didn't want to lose another piece of myself. I didn't know if I'd have anything left, as piece after piece was chipped away. Maybe the death of your body wasn't the worst outcome. It was the death of your soul.

I thought I'd found a place in the world, a weird awkward place, but a niche. I'd started to care for people. And just when I started to think I might have gotten the hang of this life, I got knocked on my ass again. But it hadn't all been a loss. I knew the lines I couldn't cross now and I knew the things I'd sacrifice. This line was thick, black and ugly and I wasn't going to cross it, no matter what they said.

"You aren't asking them to do anything you haven't already done yourself," Cormac said as I stood silently; he had his cold mask in place but it slipped just a bit when he talked. I could see the anger there.

"With one huge difference, it was my choice."

Dodd looked down. Burrom didn't care and it was clear. Rogo looked angry I was dragging this out. Vitor? Yeah, he was still looking half-dead.

"I won't vote for this."

"We need this. I'm not leaving until she votes for it," Rogo said.

"Neither am I," Dodd added.

I saw a flicker in Cormac's eyes. Would he back me? Is this, right here, the very thing I was looking for from him? I knew he cared about me...or did. I knew he cared about his people, but could I be with someone that could steam roll over every other thing without a twinge of guilt? Please, let it be a flicker of remorse over what we were going to force people to do or a spark that I still mattered to him.

His face shut down again as I watched. "You know the rules. You're in the room, you vote."

I grabbed another bottle of booze and headed toward the door. "Then I'll leave the room."

"It doesn't work that way!" Rogo yelled out.

I paused by the door. "Make it work or don't, but you're going to have to do it without me." And then I left to go drink the night away on the roof. It was Cormac's garden refuge, but whatever. He was busy with a meeting, anyway.

CHAPTER FIFTEEN

"What are you doing up here?" Cormac asked from somewhere behind me.

I waved the bottle in the air above my head as I sat on the ledge, my feet dangling over the side.

"You're afraid of heights," he stated as he walked toward the ledge.

"Yes, *I* am, but..." I paused to read the label on the bottle I held, "Mr. Glen Livet doesn't seem to mind them."

"No rippers out tonight?"

"I told them to go away."

"Nice trick. I don't know which version of Jo I prefer, the one that doesn't give a shit about anyone and is a one women machine, or the Jo that has found some calling to protect the innocents."

"I know I'd prefer the Cormac that doesn't

speak right now."

"I'm going to do what I have to..."

"Yeah, yeah...I've heard," I said, cutting him off midsentence. "And the truth is, I get it. I understand why we're doing this. Still doesn't make it right."

"I didn't come up here to fight. We decided to try doing volunteers first. I just wanted to let you know."

My fuzzy brain was trying to tell me that he was handing me an olive branch but I was too drunk to care. "We're you always like this?"

"Like what?" he asked, hands in his pockets. He was standing a few feet from me and didn't look as if he planned on coming any closer.

"Cold." I asked in the pretense of the conversation but deep down it was personal.

"When you live as long as I have, it happens. It's not something that you choose, and it's not something that happens overnight, but it happens. So no, I don't flinch at making these decisions."

I looked out at the expanse of the destruction, illuminated by the full moon. It was a scene I'd helped create. I couldn't look at the devastation without remembering my part in it. Each crumpled building on the horizon added to my burden of guilt.

"Does it bother you? Being cold like this?" Anger and resentment bled into my words.

"No, it's easier."

"But not when it comes to your people. Then

you care." People that I still wasn't a part of, or he wouldn't have been able to walk away from me so easily.

"Everyone has their weaknesses," he said.

I felt I'd been discarded pretty easily. Did I care about how he treated humans, or was I more selfish and angry about how he treated me? That I couldn't seem to stop myself from wanting him, even now, bothered me as much as the destruction hundreds of feet below.

"I'm going with the search party looking for Sabrina," I said in my best authoritative voice, changing the subject. It would have sounded a lot better if I hadn't accented it with a hiccup.

"Fine, you can come with me. The group is leaving here at seven tomorrow morning."

"You're going? Who's going to keep things in order here?"

"Dodd."

"No way Dodd is going to stay behind."

"I've already talked to him. He's not immune to the rippers, but I am. He'll be dead weight to us and he knows it."

It made sense, but even in my blurred thought process, I was taken aback. "How are you so sure that *you're* immune?"

"When you got back the other night, I took a little stroll."

Before I could ask another question, he walked away.

"Don't fall off the ledge," were his parting

words as I listened to his retreating footsteps.

CHAPTER SIXTEEN

We'd taken the trucks this time but left them about five miles shy of where we had found Colleen. We all agreed that approaching on foot felt safer than a truck, which would be spotted quicker.

"I'm just saying..." Dark paused and I saw him look back to make sure there was enough distance between us and the *changed* humans to be sure they couldn't overhear, "this doesn't look like the pick of the litter," he finished saying.

I'd initially thought the same thing myself, when I first saw the two humans that volunteered to come with us this morning. They had been surprisingly friendly toward me, which was the first thing I'd found alarming.

Dodd had been giving Dark such an interrogation about what he wanted him to do that it had delayed the entire group. Cormac had then got involved, since Dark would've sat there and listened to Dodd's instructions for hours. While they had been doing their thing, I'd gotten to know Chip and Katie.

"They're perfectly suited for what we need," I said.

"How's that?" Dark asked.

"Chip, that's the tall lanky guy in his mid-forties with the sandy colored hair. Chip is his nickname. He was a computer whiz before the shattering."

"How is that going to help?"

"Hey, Chip?" I called over the short expanse.

"Yeah?"

"Do you know where we are?"

"Latitude 36° 14' 32.442 by Longitude 115° 7' 4.8072."

"Thanks!"

"How did he do that?" Dark asked.

"When he changed, his brain started taping into the satellites that are still in orbit around the planet."

"Can he track people?" Dark asked.

"He thinks so. We've got a picture of Sabrina with us. I don't know how much juice it uses, so I wanted to wait until we got closer to where we found Colleen before we tried it out."

"Can the other one do anything?" he asked, eyeing them up with a new appreciation.

"The little strawberry blond used to be a gymnastics teacher."

"She looks like a pixie."

I nodded.

"Katie?"

"Yeah, Jo?" she answered.

"Can you show Dark a little demo?"

Her face lit up the moment I asked, clearly pleased to use her new talent and my heart swelled a little, just glad that there was some happiness in the midst of all of this.

She leapt about twenty feet in the air, did a few spins and landed gracefully on her feet.

"She didn't make a sound. If we do find them, she should be useful surveillance. She's been testing out her skills. Says she can jump about forty feet without making any noise."

As much as I got a good feeling about these two humans, I didn't know if I completely trusted the *changed*. Come on, they were changing and no one had any idea when that changing would stop. But I wasn't sharing that part. Plus, this trip was more about recon than anything else.

"That's awesome," Dark said, as we started moving again. "What's the deal with Cormac and you?"

I wasn't surprised he asked: I'd been waiting for this question. Cormac was barely acknowledging me these days. You'd have to be dumb or blind not to notice that our relationship had taken a nose dive.

"We aren't getting along," I replied stating the obvious.

"Yeah, that much is clear. What's his beef?"

"I really don't want to get into it. We just don't see eye to eye. To be honest, once this is done and over with, I might try and go out on my own." I just didn't know where.

"You'll never be able to."

"Why? There are probably other communities out there, somewhere." It was my turn to look back now and make sure no one could hear. "If he didn't own the casino, it would be different."

"No, I didn't mean you couldn't. I meant he'll never let you."

"You're wrong. He doesn't want me here." I switched the pack I was carrying to my left shoulder, the weight starting to become a nuisance, now that we'd been on the road for a while.

"Then why's he having you watched again?"

"What are you talking about?" I asked Dark, startled by the question.

"You didn't notice? I figured you knew."

"Are you sure?"

"Positive. He told everyone on watch duty to alert him immediately if you tried to leave. I know you were drunk last night, but do you really think I wanted to sit there all night making sure you didn't fall off the ledge? He's watching you like a hawk."

I looked up ahead to where Cormac was walking and I couldn't decide which emotion would win. Part of me, just the tiniest part, was a little happy that he cared if I left. The other part was pissed. He dumped me and still wanted to dictate how I came and went? And why did he care?

I wasn't going to ask him. If I decided to leave, it would be easier if he thought I didn't know, so I stewed in silence as we kept on our way.

Just like the last time, by time we got to the place we'd found Colleen, it was fully dark.

"You ready, Chip?" Cormac asked.

"Let's give it a go." Chip had a sort of nerdy gait as he walked closer to Cormac.

"Hold this." Cormac said as he handed Dark his flashlight and dug the picture of Sabrina out of his bag. We didn't have pictures of anyone else. We were lucky we had the one of Sabrina. When the storms had been tearing down their homes, no one had had time to pack pictures or anything else that hadn't been an immediate need.

"I've never tried a stranger before," Chip said nervously as he hesitated to look at the picture.

"We've got nothing to lose," I told him, trying to relieve some of the stress he was under. Some people thrive under stress. Chip appeared to be in the group that flailed.

He nodded and stepped forward, saddened by the truth of my words. "If this works, don't speak to me once I start, just follow me. Tapping into the satellites uses everything I have."

"Do it. We'll follow your lead." I laid a hand on Chip's arm. "We've got your back."

I was immediately distracted when I heard an extremely low-pitched growl. It was there and gone in a second. I looked around to locate the source, as we all did.

"What the hell was that?" I asked before I thought better of it. The humans were already skittish, making a big deal of this would just set them more on edge.

"It was nothing," Cormac said.

I turned, at first thinking he too wanted to not frighten Chip and Katie but I caught a glimmer in his eyes and a slight tensing in his muscles. It was Cormac? What the hell was going on with him, these days?

"Look at the picture," Cormac said to Chip, his voice slightly huskier than normal.

Katie and Chip knew something was wrong with him. I could see it in their movements, as they both tensed. They were scared of him. They felt it as well. I shouldn't have been surprised they sensed something was off, but I was. They were no longer just humans.

"Chip, can you do this?" I asked in the most authoritative voice I could muster. I needed to take over and get him back on track. "Chip!" I said even firmer when he didn't answer initially. "Can you do this or not?"

"Yeah," he said.

The second he took the picture, I knew I had control back.

Chip looked down at the photo and his eyes glazed over. A minute later, he started heading north again, with us all on his heels. Katie and Dark hung closer to Chip and although I didn't want too much space between me and them, I had to get a handle on Cormac.

"What the hell was that?"

"Nothing," he replied, cool and calm as if he hadn't growled like an animal a few minutes ago.

"That was *not* nothing."

"It's under control. Let it go."

He wasn't giving an inch, stubborn bastard. "Now who can't function as a team?" I threw in his face and walked off, hoping whatever issue he was having, he could keep it under control.

I left him walking behind us and double-timed it back to the group. Chip was moving at a pretty good pace and I could see his eyes still looked vacant as I got close.

Little Katie fell into place beside me. "I'm friends with Colleen," she said. "It's why I wanted to help. Do you think she's going to be okay?"

"I do."

"You can tell?"

"No...I can't *tell* any more than you can," I said, wondering what she meant by that.

"Oh. I'd heard things that made me think you could," she replied, disappointed.

"Sorry." It was the first time I'd ever had to apologize for not being freakish enough.

"What about Cormac? Does he know?"

"No, he can't tell."

"I went to the seer. She didn't know either."

"The seer?"

"Yeah, you ever been? She's good. She knew I'd be going with you."

Or made her decide to come, I thought to myself. Now we had people running around pretending to be psychic. But then again, maybe they were. I had to keep reminding myself this wasn't the world it used to be. Actually, the old world wasn't what I'd thought it had been, either.

Things were changing so rapidly it was becoming hard to keep track of all the comings and goings at the casino. I wanted to ask Cormac if he'd heard about the seer but we were hardly on idle chit chat terms. Plus, he was keeping his distance from the group, right now. I, on the other hand, couldn't. Until the rippers showed up and I knew for sure they wouldn't bother them, I wasn't comfortable leaving too much space between them and me.

I was just about to answer no when out of nowhere I tripped. I thought I snagged my foot on a vine somehow until I heard the softest little giggle by my ear and a flashing that looked like a few lightning bugs zig-zag away.

"You okay?" Katie asked. The rest of the group was looking around at what happened.

"Yeah, just caught a shrub I didn't see."

Of course, they all had to flash their lights at the ground having some sort of compulsion to locate the nefarious shrub.

"Must have been a rock," I said when the evil shrub didn't come into view. "We're losing Chip," I continued.

"What was that?" Cormac asked, catching up.

"That was me tripping." I brushed off my pants and started walking forward.

Cormac, appeased and looking a bit calmer, headed to the front of the group. It allowed me to hang back a bit, hoping to go unnoticed so I could figure out what just happened. As soon as there was some distance between the group and me, the bugs started flitting around in view again. In the dark night, they looked exactly like lightning bugs, but lightning bugs didn't giggle.

"Hello?" I said softly, thinking I was crazy for even trying to greet lightning bugs.

"Hi, Jo!" excited little helium sounding voices chimed out.

"Did you trip me?"

Little giggles filled the air near my ear. "Not on purpose. We like your boots. We didn't mean to trip you."

"It wasn't nice to giggle at me falling," I told them in a hushed whisper. A year ago I would've been in freak out mode over hearing lightning bugs speak; these days weird was old hat.

A sad little chorus of "awww" escaped them in unison.

"What are you?" I asked, walking now but keeping a certain distance from everyone else.

"We're lightning bugs, Jo," one of them said.

I looked at the group of them flying around my head. They did look like lightning bugs. "Lightning bugs don't talk."

A collective "Hmmm," went through the little group, as if I'd stumped them. A rough count showed eight bugs in total, flying around

One of them did a kamikaze dive an inch away from my face. "Look at me, Jo! I can turn pink! Hehehe."

"How do you know my name?"

"Cuz you're Jo!" they said. "Yeah, you're Jo!"

That explained nothing as I kept pace with the group, close enough for no one to be concerned but far enough that I hoped no one was noticing what was going on. I couldn't believe I'd never considered that magic might have an effect on other things besides humans.

I watched the tail of the talking bug turn pink instead of yellow. "Oh no, the scary one's coming back," another one of them said.

"He's okay," I told them as I watched Cormac approach.

"Oh no! Got to go. Have to hide!" They started flying in frenzied circles.

"Why?"

"We know things! We can read. We know the rules. We saw that big sign. What happens in Vegas stays in Vegas. We don't want to break the law."

"That's not what it means," I tried to explain but they were whizzing around frantically.

"Oh no, Jo. We've got to go. Rules. Got to go!" I watched the lightning bugs fly off as Cormac approached.

"What are you doing?" he asked as he stood a few feet from me in black cargo pants and a t-shirt.

The lightning bugs were gone. "Would you believe it if I said I was talking to bugs?"

"Stop screwing around. This isn't a joke. You shouldn't be hanging this far back by yourself." He turned on his heels and started walking off.

I quickly caught up to him. "And you should keep your distance from the humans, because you're scary." I kept walking past and threw back, "The bug whisperer has it under control. We don't need you," over my shoulder.

I heard his laughter as I moved closer to the group and it almost felt like we were back to our old bickering, but nothing was the same.

It was eerily silent and dark. No rippers, no people. Chip marched ahead at his own personal beat and I wondered, more than once, what he was seeing in his mind's eye.

We slogged along through the night. The only one that seemed fresh as we continued was Cormac. He was lingering about ten feet behind us, perhaps taking my scary comments to heart and trying not to alarm Katie and Chip.

The rippers didn't stay at bay completely. They would occasionally dodge in and out, but they didn't bother anyone. They would just check us out as they passed by. Except for me. They were more interested in me, for some reason, and I had to tell them to leave more than once. It didn't work the first time I said it, I had to wait until I got mad or got stressed or just got ...more. That's when the mist would come out. Without the mist, my words were ordinary. But even with the mist, they wouldn't go away completely.

We hadn't seen anything in a while and when I first saw the sparkling ahead in the dark, I thought nothing of it. I knew it was the bugs and I thought they were just playing. But something about the way they were circling over the one spot started to alarm me.

I ran to the front and stopped everyone in their tracks, jolting Chip out of his trance in the process. Cormac was by my side before I even had a chance to look for him. He silently motioned to a knoll about twenty feet from where we stood.

"What is it?" Cormac asked once we had some cover.

"There's something wrong up ahead. Chip, any idea?" I asked, wondering how much he could see.

"I can't tell, but it isn't Sabrina. She's about five miles north of here."

"I'll go ahead and check it out," I said. "You guys wait here."

"Like hell, you will. I'll go, you wait," Cormac said.

"I should go," Katie's high voice said, breaking our standoff. "I'm the quietest one here and the most nimble. I'll go over there and see what's up and then come right back."

Cormac and I met each other's stare for a moment. "Fine," we both said in unison.

Katie just smiled and nodded. We watched as she danced along, staying close to the ground and moving from shadow to shadow until she was practically on top of the area where the lightning bugs hovered.

"She's getting very close," I whispered to Cormac. "What's she doing?" I started to jump up but Cormac grabbed my arm, dragging me back down beside him. I was about to argue when I saw Chip's face look to Cormac and then me. I think he was as scared of being left alone with Cormac as he was of whatever was out there, so I held my breath and waited.

I stayed crouched where I was as I saw her get closer and closer. When her scream hit the air, my patience ran out. I jumped out from behind the knoll and sprinted toward her, but Cormac was there before I even took three steps. How the hell did he get there that fast?

He put a hand over her mouth as he ran back toward us, carrying her in his other arm. I should've been thinking only of what she'd just found, but I couldn't get past how he'd gotten there so quickly. And really, what was the point of the charade of running back?

"Hold her," he said, practically shoving a still shaking Katie into my arms.

"Here," I said as I then shoved Katie at Chip, who didn't look much better. Great special ops team we made.

Whatever was out there, I needed to know.

Cormac jogged back toward the spot as I followed on his heels.

He didn't say a word as I stopped beside him and looked down at what had upset Katie so much. If I'd been a religious type, I would've said the devil lay there before us. Only issue with that notion was, the devil was the one who usually did the torturing.

The dead man's legs and arms looked mangled. That alone might not have meant torture but I nudged Cormac and pointed to the guy's fingers. Every single one had been broken.

"He's one of ours," I said as I squatted down close enough to make out his face. His name was James and he'd been on the senator's list. "And now we know why he never took off that cowboy hat."

Three-inch long nubs that looked like they would've eventually grown into horns were visible as they poked through his hair. His hat lay a few feet from his body.

"I hear something," Cormac said a second before a tiny pinprick of light appeared in the west, heading right for where Katie, Chip and Dark were.

I took off in their direction and I heard Cormac following behind me. And then in a flash, we were standing there with them and I had no idea how we'd gotten there.

I looked at Cormac but he wasn't paying any attention to me. All his attention was for the double set of headlights that were barreling down on us, as two large Hummers pulled to a stop in front, kicking up dust. There was no point in running now.

"Throw down your weapons," a deep voice called out.

"Why the hell should..." I started to yell back until the sounds of arms being thrown to the ground disrupted my thoughts. I understood why Dark would do it. He didn't need them. As soon as he switched form, he'd be able to rip them apart with his bare hands, but why would the other two do it?

All I could hear from Cormac was an outward sigh of annoyance.

I turned around for a second, knowing it wasn't going to make the slightest difference to the outcome, threw my hands up and rolled my eyes. "Really, people? You couldn't even wait for him to ask twice?"

I'd like to think they looked ashamed, but in all honesty, they looked more terrified than anything else.

Cormac was beside me, slightly angled in front but with the way the trucks were parked, it was impossible to completely block me. Looking ahead, I couldn't see much with the lights in my face, but I heard boots hit the ground. Two vehicles meant at least two drivers but we all knew there wouldn't be just a pair.

The silhouette of a large male form stepped forward in front of the trucks. I couldn't see anything but an outline of his body with a fire arm strapped to his side. The fact that it was still in its holster wasn't reassuring. It simply meant that there were enough others trained on us that he didn't feel the need.

"Drop your arms," a deep voice said to Cormac and me; everyone else already had.

"Why don't you tell me who you are?" Cormac replied, taking a step forward.

"We..." the dark silhouette started speaking and then several things happened simultaneously.

The sounds of bullets whizzed through the air, and a sharp piercing pain hit my shoulder just as I was shoved to the ground and covered by Cormac.

"Stop!"

I heard the shout as I was eating a mouth full of dirt. I was pretty sure it was the silhouetted man that had given the order but I couldn't see. I could just feel the wound and it burned like crazy.

The bullets stopped and it was dead silent again.

"Are you okay?" Cormac asked.

"I'm fine."

And then he was gone, and Katie was by my side. "Jo?" she asked.

"It's okay."

"Stand down!" The still unnamed man shouted to his men as I watched Cormac pin him to the hood of one of the trucks, his forearm pressing on his throat.

"Help me get up," I said to Katie and she

grabbed my good arm. I looked at my torn shirt but it was black so the blood and hole from the bullet wasn't easy to spot. I didn't know how long it would take to heal but I wasn't going to sit there, looking all injured, while we were outnumbered.

Seven men, all in army fatigues, swarmed out of the truck, circling Cormac and the man he had pinned.

"My name is Crash. We don't want you, we want our people." The guy's voice was strained from Cormac's forearm pressed against his throat.

"Tell your guys to stand down," Cormac told him.

"Do it," Crash ordered.

"Who shot the girl there?" Cormac demanded.

"I did," one of the guys said in a "what are you gonna do about it" tone.

Cormac released Crash and was over to him and laid him out before anyone knew what was happening.

"Leave it," Crash said to his men. "He deserved it. He had no order to fire."

Something struck me as off about the explanation, but I couldn't put my finger on it. Maybe it simply wasn't how I would have handled it.

"Who are you?" I asked as Cormac made his way back over from the still unconscious man.

"We're looking for Oslo. We received word he was on his way back and then he disappeared," Crash said.

He knew we'd recognize the name. He already knew who we were.

"They're with the senator," Cormac said, midstride, with a sneer.

"It's nice to meet you, Jo," Crash said. "And I can only assume this is Cormac."

Crash made a hand motion and the headlights turned off, leaving a dimmer illumination from the fog lights. His people all looked like they'd just returned from a war, crew cuts and all.

Crash held up his hand and signaled for his people to wait where they were, as he approached Cormac and me.

"We aren't looking for trouble. We only want our people," Crash said, once he got a few feet away.

"They aren't your people," Cormac said, taking a step closer to Crash.

"Look," he said, dropping his tone. "I've got a job to do. We received notice from Oslo that he was on his way back with ten willing companions. No one forced them to come. They disappeared before they made it back to the checkpoint. I'm assuming you are out here trying to find them as well."

Neither of us denied it, which was basically an agreement.

"Wherever they are now, it's not their choice. I've got an offer," Crash said.

Cormac was brewing and Crash was waiting for an answer so I jumped to grab the olive branch.

"We're listening," I said.

"We find them together, get them out and let them make their own choice from there."

I saw Cormac's mouth shape into a no and cut him off before he could speak. "Give us a minute." I signaled our group over while Crash went back to his people.

"I don't like this guy," Cormac said the second we were out of earshot.

"We don't have a choice."

"Your shoulder still hurt?" Cormac asked, eyeing me up.

I immediately dropped the hand that had unconsciously been holding it. I knew my shoulder would heal on its own, but it was still burning like crazy. I didn't want anyone else to know. They didn't need distractions.

"No, already closing." It wasn't. I could feel trickles of blood dripping as I stood there, but I'd tell him when we were alone and away from the humans. By that point, it would probably have closed anyway.

"We've got to work with them."

"Absolutely not," Cormac said.

"Sabrina and the rest of them are close. Crash and his people are heading in the right direction. They could potentially beat us there. So, I repeat, we don't have a choice."

Cormac was so aggravated by the idea, he didn't even remember to shutter his expression, or maybe he just didn't care who saw the anger in his eyes. It normally annoyed me when his face was a mask. This time, I wished he'd mute it down.

Chip was getting more skittish by the minute and we needed him functioning. Katie, on the other hand, was proving to be quite tough. This was a girl that I could get along with and I needed some more estrogen around. Without Sabrina, I was drowning in manliness. Plus, she was small. I was sick of arching my neck to talk to everyone.

"I agree with Jo," Katie said.

Oh yeah, Katie and I were definitely going to get along.

"Sabrina and Oslo weren't slouches. Whoever took them had some power," I said, seeing a little momentum building.

"Then we'll bring more muscle."

"Private word?" I asked Cormac as I walked a bit further away from Katie, Chip and Dark. Cormac followed me over. "I don't know exactly what you're capable of, especially *now.*" I didn't elaborate, knowing he knew exactly what I was talking about. "But it's pointless. Even if we get them out of there alone, if they're determined to go to the senator, they will."

"I won't let her."

It saddened me a bit that the only one he cared about was Sabrina, but there wasn't much I could do. "You can't lock her up and you know it. All we'll be doing is exhausting much needed manpower."

"Fine. We'll do it your way, but I don't like it."

I turned and nodded to Dark, instinctively knowing he'd understand and explain to the others as we called Crash over.

"We go in together, but I run the show," Cormac said,

I cleared my throat. "We run the show," I corrected.

"Why do you get to?" Crash asked.

"Cause we know the location. It's our game, we're just letting you play," Cormac replied.

"This isn't dodgeball, people," I added.

"Okay," Crash said. I saw a hint of a smile on Crash's face and that was it...I knew something was off. The guy was just too damn agreeable. This was not someone looking for a fight. How did he get to be in the position of leading this group? Crash glanced in my direction, as if he knew I was sensing something off with him, but his eyes moved on quickly.

"When we get closer to the locale, a couple of us will go ahead on foot," I said. Cormac and Crash looked at each other for a second and then nodded.

"Get in the trucks. It'll be quicker."

"Can you fit us?" I asked, looking at his guys and wondering how close I wanted to get to them.

"It'll be tight, but yes."

We split into two groups. I could tell Cormac was uneasy dividing up, but we didn't have much of a choice. Neither group wanted to be with the other, but they also weren't ready to hand over a truck.

I squeezed into the front seat of one hummer, in between Crash and one of his G.I. Joe men. Chip had come with me and was squished in the back with the other guys. Dark, making a show of changing, which was so not his style, changed into wolf form and followed along on foot. A few miles were nothing to him.

We'd gotten close enough that Chip could direct us the rest of the way without having an issue. If the driver could stop hitting every bump going, it would be smooth sailing, but I wasn't so lucky. Every time we hit a bump, my shoulder slammed into Crash and pain shot down my arm. I could feel the blood still leaking out of the wound. Why hadn't it healed? Cormac and Dark would smell the blood but not think anything of it, since they'd assume any injury would already be closing.

I was positive something was very wrong with my shoulder, but I needed to suck it up and not be a wimp. We were so close to where Chip said we should be to find Sabrina. Another few minutes and we'd stop. That's what needed my attention.

As much as I wanted to take the lead, I knew Cormac and Katie were best suited. That girl moved like a cat and just as quietly. I had no description for how Cormac was moving, other than maybe *strange*. I was going to force myself to be a team player, even if it killed me.

Out of the corner of my eye, I caught Crash looking at the hole in my shirt before he noticed me watching him. I did a single shake of my head. His stare paused for a moment and then he looked away, holding his tongue. Yeah, I didn't know who Crash was, but I didn't think he was a company man.

"Here," Chip said. "It shouldn't be too far." Our Hummer pulled over to the side, closely followed by the other.

We piled out and my eyes instinctively sought Cormac as I watched the men in the other truck pile out.

"Cormac and Katie are the best people to go ahead," I said once everyone grouped together.

"I need one of my guys to go," Crash said.

"Your guys are too loud. They'll hear us coming," Cormac said.

"We'll be here, waiting with you. They won't go in alone. They'll go, check out the situation and come back," I said.

Cormac nodded his head in agreement.

"Okay," Crash said.

I watched Cormac and Katie leave in the direction Chip told them. It was hard not to be nervous. I wasn't so sure Cormac wouldn't take an opening if he saw it and then what? But there was nothing else to do but wait, as we watched them disappear into the dark.

As soon as they were completely gone, our group split into two. G.I. Joes on one side, Freaks R Us on the other. We were outnumbered, but had a lot more to work with so it felt even anyway.

My shoulder was throbbing worse than ever, but I was doing everything I could to act normal. I was just about to tell Dark and ask him to help cover for me when Crash walked over.

"Can I talk to you over on the side for a moment?" he asked, as I stood there with Dark and Chip.

"Sure," I said, not being able to think of a plausible excuse not to agree. With Crash, I'd have to pretend everything was fine.

"By the truck," he said, and motioned to where the one Hummer sat by itself. I followed him around to the other side wondering what this was all about, also knowing I could probably kill him as long as he didn't shoot me again. His guys stared curiously at both of us as we walked together. "I'd like to go over the maps with you."

We stepped over to the truck and he pulled out huge maps and held them up, blocking our view of everyone else.

"We've got to get that bullet out of your shoulder."

I looked at him warily. He already knew enough about us to identify me on sight, but I wasn't going to spell out Keeper secrets to him that he might not know. The fact that Keepers could normally heal easily from bullets wasn't something I wanted to explain. Even if this one was taking a while, it would happen soon enough.

"It's fine. It was just a graze."

"There's no exit hole in the back of your shirt."

I narrowed my eyes. "I'm fine."

"It's not going to heal."

Man, this guy was stubborn.

"I told you, I'm fine."

"I know what you are and I know what you people can do." He leaned a hair closer and spoke in slow and punctuated words. "It's not going to heal. They're not regular bullets."

I kept my face neutral as I realized I was screwed.

"Exactly," he said.

Okay, maybe I wasn't so neutral on the facial expressions. But I was afraid he was right. I could feel the wound still dripping blood. I hadn't even clotted yet. It should have stopped bleeding, at the very least.

"I can take it out."

I looked around at the dust bowl we were currently in. I'd never discussed infection with any of the Keepers, but I didn't think it was an issue.

"Why do you want to help me?" I asked, eyeing him skeptically.

"I can't answer that."

"Nothing personal, but I'd rather have one of my own people do it."

"The guy with the paws or the one that can't stop shaking? Do whatever you want, but I can't have my men knowing."

"I don't see the difference between you knowing or you and all of your men."

If the senator knew we were aware of the

bullets, he'd simply switch to something else. But what did it matter if Crash already knew? Wouldn't his men know too?

"I can't spell it out for you, but there is."

I surveyed the area. Crash's men were about twenty feet from my people. For the most part, they seemed to be chatting between themselves but I could tell a couple of them were paying attention to what we were doing, although not blatantly.

Chip and Dark were talking, but they kept glancing at us, looking concerned. If I hadn't felt so miserable, I would've laughed. They didn't realize I could kick Crash's ass, even injured. I waved them over using my good side, my left hand feeling slightly numb and cold.

Dark walked over, followed by Chip. Crash was right. There was nothing Dark was going to be able to do with those gigantic paws of his. Chip was the winner. I just hoped he could stop shaking for a couple of minutes.

"What's wrong?" Chip asked quietly as he came closer, Dark not able to speak.

"I've got a problem. There's a bullet in my shoulder and I need you to take it out," I said to Chip, and pointed to the hole in my shirt.

"Here? We're going to do it here?" Chip asked.

"Yes."

His face went from concern to horror.

"What about infection?" he asked.

"I'm not worried about that. I've got to get this

out."

"But you know we're running low on peni-"

"I'm not worried about it," I said flaring my eyes. Crash did not need to know every little nitty-gritty detail of our current survival state and the sad fact that we were low on medications.

Crash had gone out on a limb by telling me about the bullets but I didn't trust anyone that worked for the senator. Hell, sometimes I barely trusted Cormac and I'd lived with him. The last thing I wanted was for the senator to know how dire our situation was. That we were rationing food while they were driving around in fully equipped Hummers.

"Keep your men over there," I said to Crash and moved further into the shadow of the truck, Chip and Dark following me.

I pulled off my shirt, not caring who saw me in a sports bra. Blood was everywhere, and I hoped it looked worse than it was. Then I looked at Chip, his face a grayish shade.

"Come on, Chip. You can't chicken out on me. I need you to do this."

Dark let out a small growl, wordlessly asking me if he should shift back.

"No." I didn't have to explain that I didn't trust any of these men. He didn't either. We needed Dark in his most formidable shape. "Chip can do this," I said.

"What do I do?" Chip asked. He had his arms folded in front of him and I was hoping it wasn't to disguise his shaking. "Do we have something to dig it out with?"

I looked around to make sure no one was approaching. Crash was standing by himself several feet away from the truck but with a clear view of us and ready to block anyone that came over.

"I want you to stick your finger in the wound and feel for the bullet. You've got to get it out." When he started to wobble, I knew I was in bad shape. "Chip, I need you to get this thing out or my wound isn't going to close." I didn't tell him I wasn't sure if it would close even after the bullet was out. He looked unsure enough without that information.

He unfolded his arms and moved his hands closer but then pulled back. He took a breath, shook his hands a couple of times.

"Close your eyes if you have to. It's mostly feel anyway," I told him.

He nodded vigorously, moved his hand into position and shut his eyes before he stuck his fingers into my wound. I couldn't tell if he was making progress or making it worse. It's hard to tell expressions on a wolf but I could've sworn Dark was grimacing.

The minute I saw Crash shake his head, I knew he'd lost his patience with Chip muddling through this on his own. He walked over to us and stood there, waiting.

I looked at Chip's shaking hands again and relented. "Wipe the blood off your hand with my shirt and go stand over there. If anyone asks what you're doing, tell them I needed a couple of minutes of privacy."

"With them?" Chip asked, knowing how ridiculous it would look.

"Just do it."

"Okay," he said and looked relieved to not have to dig into me again.

Crash stepped closer to me and looked at my shoulder, visibly grimacing. "This is going to hurt like hell."

"It can't be worse than what Chip just did. Just do it."

"Yes, it can. He was afraid to go deep enough."

"What are you doing?" I asked when he positioned his left hand under my right arm.

"Bracing you so that you don't fall when I stick my hand into your torso."

I closed my eyes and took a deep breath, waiting to see what the new round of pain would be like. I didn't expect it to be pleasant and when the pain came, it more than met my expectations.

I don't know how, but I managed to not cry out, even though I succumbed to tears.

"Just another minute," he said, seeing my duress. "I can feel it, I just have to get a grip on it."

I didn't nod or speak.

"Get your hands off her," Cormac growled, and not quietly.

And the gig was up. Any of Crash's men that hadn't been suspicious before would be now as they all came rushing over to see what the commotion was. None of them seemed to like what they saw.

"I'm knuckle deep and touching a bullet that I need to get out. If I leave it, she's going to bleed to death," Crash explained as he neither retreated, nor proceeded, but remained completely still. The non-action didn't stop the pain caused by his fingers still being lodged in sinew.

Cormac was now on top of us and breathing down Crash's neck as he stared down at my bloodied shoulder.

"Finish," I said. "Just get it out."

No one spoke as I felt Crash's finger dig a bit deeper.

Cormac's hand grabbed my good one. I knew it was his, even with my eyes closed. Maybe more so with my eyes closed. I could feel him trying to absorb some of my pain, another cool trick he could do that I couldn't.

"I almost forgot about that," I whispered, knowing he'd realize what I meant.

"You can't be jealous. You're the bug whisperer."

I looked over at him and found myself smiling at his joke, in spite of the pain that was still ripping through me. His eyes softened back.

I could feel Crash's fingers delving into muscle and it took everything I had to not move away, although that would be difficult in my current position, with the Hummer at my back.

"One more minute and I'll have it," Crash said. "I just have to get a grip on it. It's slippery with the blood."

"Stop worrying about the damage and get it out," I said through my teeth. Whatever additional trauma to the tissue he caused would heal quickly, but this was torture.

He looked at me, gauging my seriousness. "Okay, this is gonna suck."

"It's been a pleasure, so far."

For a few seconds, it felt like he shoved his entire fist into my shoulder but then the bullet was out. He held it up, showing it had remained intact and not shattered when it hit and lodged near the bone.

"I'll take that," Cormac said to Crash as he stepped directly between the two of us.

Crash didn't move, still holding the bullet firmly in his hand.

I looked around at Crash's disgruntled looking men, who were now eyeing Crash with suspicion. He couldn't hand over the bullet in front of his guys.

"It's just a bullet," Crash said and looked at me.

He'd done me a favor and was looking for payback. I squeezed Cormac's hand trying to give him a silent clue. We didn't need this specific one anyway. They probably had boxes of ammo sitting in the back of these trucks. The only thing this would do is out Crash's blurry motives, ones that might end up being to our benefit.

"That was in her and did a hell of a lot of damage," Cormac said, not dropping the issue.

"We'll burn it," Crash offered as a compromise.

"Fine."

I looked around at the group and realized everyone seemed to accept that compromise pretty well.

Dark pulled together a few tumbleweeds that would make a quick fire and burn out quickly. Crash threw the bullet onto it.

"If you don't mind?" Cormac asked, looking at Crash's blood soaked hand.

"Pete? Get me the whiskey out of the truck."

A minute later, my blood was removed from Crash's hand and the bullet charred. We could finally get back to the matter at hand.

"What did you find?" I asked.

Cormac dug into his zipped pocket and dug out his funny phone. He was in stone-faced mode again but Katie blanched. It told me how bad it was before either of them uttered a word, maybe telling me more than I wanted to know.

"Yours has a camera?" I asked. I'd been carrying around this lousy phone that looked like it came from the eighties. I knew I should've been happy that Cormac had rigged up a cell service, but it was hard not to be aghast that there had been a funny phone upgrade and no one had bothered to tell me. When had fs, funnyphone with good shit, hit the market?

"We'll discuss phones later, Jo," Cormac

replied in a serious manner, but I saw the underlying laughter and mockery. His expression was screaming *ha ha ha, I've got a better phone*.

Cormac held up his phone, showing a grainy picture of the buildings. "They're in a large generator plant, not far from here."

I knew I shouldn't say anything. I tried to stop myself, knowing it wasn't the time or the place, but the words slipped out anyway. "Is that like...two megapixels?"

Cormac looked up at me, glaring slightly.

Yeah, that's right, buddy, I said it. Your camera phone isn't all that.

"Did you see any of them? Oslo or the others?" Crash asked, bringing the conversation back to subject.

"No, but there's a lot of people there," Katie said. "And other things."

Cormac handed me his phone and I flipped through the images while we all crowded around the small screen.

It looked like there were guards on walkways on top of the buildings. The place was lit, but it was a generator plant. Who knew how large of a coal stash they had. It was a good site to pick, with the large body of water behind it.

And then I saw the rippers. That wouldn't be out of the ordinary except that something seemed off. They weren't scattered along the area but clumped together.

"Why are they gathered like that?" I asked,

looking at the pictures. They appeared to be in a frenzied swarm.

Everyone looked up, wondering the same thing as me. Even in the dark, I could see Katie had turned white.

"They were feeding," Cormac said.

"Did you see who they caught? Was it one of their people or ours?"

"They didn't catch anything, they were fed."

CHAPTER SEVENTEEN

"What are those men doing with you? Who are they?" Buzz asked.

"Not here," I said. I looked behind me at the casino lobby where Cormac was telling Kever where to put Crash and his men. I motioned to the stairwell, which was becoming my place.

I should have known something was up as I saw the door to the stairs open and let out a group of people. When had everyone started taking the stairs?

When I entered the stairwell, it was like Grand Central Station, people coming and going every second or so. I had to press myself against the wall to let an especially large group get by. "What the hell?"

"The elevators on this side of the casino are gone," Buzz explained.

"They broke?"

"Uh, no, not broke. Just gone."

"Gone where? Talk, Buzz!" I said, losing more and more patience as I saw my stairwell becoming completely overrun.

"Last night, at approximately two a.m. they disappeared."

I looked at him, almost not believing what he was saying. He threw his hands into the air and shrugged.

"What's there now?"

"Stone. It was pretty ugly. A couple of people were in them when they disappeared and they got wedged in between the stone walls. It was a disaster to get them out."

"Are the Fae behind it? We need to figure out who's screwing around. This is not the time for practical jokes."

"They are denying any involvement."

Tired of being bumped by the people passing by, I entered the flow of traffic heading upward with Buzz. It looked like I'd have to get used to sharing my stairwell. Even though there were other elevators in the casino, no one would want to use them, now.

The crowd dissipated the higher up we got and I was able to start taking the stairs two at a time by the tenth floor.

"If it's not the Fae, then what's happening to the building?" I said as soon as we had enough privacy.

"Burrom is starting to think it's the spells they've been using toward the casino. He wouldn't tell me the whole thing, but there is at least one line in the incantation that says something about being as strong as a fortress of yore. The way he explained it, now that magic is much stronger, it could be interpreting the words more literally."

"Fortress of yore? With all the crazy shit happening these days and stone popping up everywhere, it just occurred to them?" As bizarre of an idea as it was, it was a logical conclusion, considering the progression of things. "Does he have any guess as to how much of a castle we are to become?"

"Nope. Did you find Sabrina and the rest of the *changed*? Dodd is climbing the walls. I think he might lose it soon."

"We found them but they're being held at a heavily armed generator plant."

"Shit. How many?"

"That's one of the problems. It's not just the *changed*. They've got rippers there and they seem to be in cahoots, somehow. I don't know if the rippers are bright enough to make a deal with or maybe they're just tamed somehow. Whatever is going on, it's not good."

"What do you mean?"

"They're feeding them."

"What?"

I didn't say anything as I waited for him to absorb this new information. His face contorted into horror. "How could they do that? They're still human."

I just shook my head, having no words for it.

It took a minute for Buzz to get over the shock himself before he moved on to the next issue. "What are those guys doing here?"

"They're with the senator."

"This day just keeps getting better and better."

"No one wanted to go in unprepared and we also didn't want them going in without us, or vice versa, so we hit a stalemate. Problem is, neither one of us wants to lose sight of the other." I looked back at Buzz, who was starting to lose ground to me on the stairs and I waited for a minute, so I didn't have to yell. Once he caught up again, I continued. "So we got stuck with them."

Buzz nodded. "Oh, and before I forget, Burrom's been waiting for you."

"Do you know what he wants?" I lived on his floor so what was the big rush?

"Said it was a private matter."

My plan was to stay on Crash's group like white on rice, but Burrom wasn't someone I felt comfortable leaving hanging.

"Can you do me a favor?"

Buzz nodded.

"Don't let the tall one with the sandy hair out of your sight. He's not what he seems and I want to know what the deal is."

"Where you going?"

"Burrom," I said, breaking into a run as I

cleared the final stairs, leaving Buzz behind.

"Change your shirt first!" he yelled after me and I remembered what a mess I was.

After Crash removed the bullet from my shoulder, the pain had subsided quickly. I got into my room, wiped down the old blood and changed my shirt before I headed back out.

I opened the door and headed down the hallway to find Burrom. He was already in his suite, waiting.

"You alone?" he asked, his eyes darting around me as I walked in.

"Yes."

"Lock it," he said, motioning to his door.

I did as he asked and the moment it shut, his pretense dropped and I could see the strain appear in his face.

"What's wrong with you?" I asked as I followed him into the living room, where I watched him collapse upon the couch.

"It's time for me to go to ground."

"Now?" I asked. His eyes closed, feet up on the couch, all I was waiting for was to hear a death rattle.

"Tonight."

"You can't go tonight. You said there was some time! I don't know how to do anything, yet!"

"This isn't a choice. I've got to go to ground."

I waited for more of an explanation that didn't come. He was lying so still with his eyes closed I wasn't even sure if he was breathing. "Burrom?"

His eyes opened again and he turned his head. "The magic is too strong. It's calling me back to the ground early. I've got to go."

"And that's it? You get a day's notice?"

"No, there have been signs but it was so early, I thought I was mistaken."

"Cormac's coming." He dragged himself to his feet.

"So what? He knows most of this anyway."

"I don't want him coming and knowing where I'm buried. He'll use it, if needed." He grabbed his pipe and walked to his door. "Meet me in the stairwell landing, seventh floor, at eleven tonight. That should be enough time. Tell no one!"

"But where are you going? This is your place?"

"I don't want to see him. He won't care. He's here to check up on you, anyway."

He held out his hand to shake mine. It was an odd gesture, but he was an odd little creature. I shook his hand and watched him leave.

He zipped out and I thought he was wrong when I heard nothing for a good five minutes. Then Cormac strolled in by himself. I looked exhausted, like usual, but not him. His clothes were a bit dirty and dusty from the road, but other than that, he looked like he'd just woken from an afternoon nap.

"Where is everyone?" I asked, curious to see him alone and on the seventh floor.

"Keeping an eye on the senator's men."

"What are you doing here?"

"I wanted to speak to Burrom," he said, but

Burrom wasn't here and he didn't look like he was leaving. "What are you doing here?"

"I live down the hall now, remember?"

He stalked me across the room, not stopping until he was so close I could feel the heat of him. I saw his eyes rest on my shoulder.

"Totally healed," I said and stepped away from him. He didn't get to dump me, kick me out of what I'd come to consider my home and then act all worried.

His eyes lost their look of concern and grew deadly serious.

"Why didn't you tell me you had a problem?"

"Because, maybe, I didn't want to announce to everyone that I was wounded."

He took a couple steps toward me, following me across the room. "You should've pulled me aside."

"When? While you were ignoring me or when you were giving me dirty looks? You weren't exactly receptive to talking to me."

"Don't bring personal matters into this. I would've listened to you. You were jeopardizing our situation. What if we had gone in? Then what? You wouldn't have been able to perform and I wouldn't have known until you got us all killed?"

It had been better when I thought he'd cared. Now that I knew it was all business, I was furious. "I would've been fine. Just get out." I didn't scream. If he was going to be cold, I wouldn't give him the luxury of seeing how this was tearing me apart inside.

"What?" he said, as if he doubted what I'd said.

"Get. Out."

Instead of leaving, he came closer and towered over me. "This is my casino."

"Fine. I'll see this thing through with Sabrina and then I'll leave."

"Where?"

"It doesn't matter. I'll find somewhere but I'm not going to stay here, not like this." Not so close to someone that ripped my heart apart, with either his anger or his indifference, every time I saw him.

"You aren't going anywhere," he replied, like he had a choice in the matter. Then he had the balls to say, "That's not your decision."

"Whose is it then? It's not yours. You can't even look at me, most of the time. You should be happy. You wanted me out."

"You're right, I do. But unfortunately, we need you and as long as we do, you aren't going anywhere."

"You're insane. You want me out but now I can't leave?"

"Yes, that's right." He turned with no explanation and I watched him leave the room.

"And I'm the crazy one?" I yelled at his back. It didn't matter what he said, I'd leave when I was ready.

CHAPTER EIGHTEEN

"Why are we on a golf course?" I asked. I'd imagined a lot of weird places I might have to go to help Burrom, but one of the more well known golf courses, not far from the Vegas Strip, wasn't anything I'd ever considered.

"Because I'm not completely certain how much control you have of your strength. I want to do it someplace you can return to easily, just in case you botch it."

I watched as he moved around the golf course, laying hands on trees here and there.

"Hey, before you go under...or wherever it is you do, can you tell me if there's anything odd about this bullet?"

He turned from the trees he was inspecting and made a slight grunting noise under his breath, but he held out his hand. I dug the bullet out of my pocket that I'd lifted from the G.I. Joes' truck the other night and handed it to him.

I watched as his fingers toyed with it for a minute or so. "It's spelled and by someone very strong."

"Yeah, that would most likely be the senator," I'd hoped it had been a fluke and the bullet might of just hit in such a way that my body wasn't able to expel it.

"It fits. It's dark magic," Burrom said.

"Like his dark smoke probably is."

"Exactly like the smoke." He handed me back the bullet too quickly, as if he didn't like the feel of it in his grasp. "Did you bring the knife?"

"Yes," I said and reached down to my ankle where I had started to wear a holster.

"I'm going to teach you a phrase. Then I will go beneath the ground. You need to slice your vein and dribble a steady stream of blood in a five feet radius around this tree. Not gushing, but a bit more than a trickle. Then you will repeat the phrase."

"How will I know if it worked?"

"You will."

That sounded ominous.

"I need you to come here every year on this day for the next fifty years and repeat the process."

"Every year? What if I'm dead or not around here?" I asked, overwhelmed by the obligation he was laying on me.

"Normally it would only be every five, but I'll

have no way of knowing how strongly your magic is progressing, so you need to come more often. If you're dead, that can't be helped. If you aren't in the area, I suggest you plan a trip."

"What if I can't?"

"Then you better hope you're dead when I reawaken." He started to slowly pace around the tree, holding out his arm as if there was a trickle of blood dripping. "You need to repeat these words, 'Seal this ground from all who come.'"

"It's in English?" My first magical spell and I was kind of hoping for something with more flair.

"You can say it in any language you want. You don't know Ground Fae, so I was giving you the translation. It's the words in conjunction with your magic and blood that will make it work. Can I continue now?"

"No reason to be testy. I just want to make sure I'm doing it right. I've never done magic before."

"Yes, you have."

"By accident. That doesn't count."

He shook his head and started to trail around again. "The words must be said in one circle of the area and one ring of the tree. 'Seal this ground from all who come. Repel all bearing ill will and death to those who dare to trespass'."

"That's it?"

"Yes. Are you ready?"

"I guess?"

Burrom walked toward the tree and stood

above the ground.

"Wait! What do I do if it doesn't work?"

"It will."

"What if it doesn't?"

"Then, and only then, can you get Cormac. He'll know how to fix it. I'll deal with the cost when I awake next."

"If he's strong enough to do this and knows how...why me? Because I'm free?"

"The magic wants you. The cards told me. And don't ask me why. Magic isn't always logical, but it's often very decisive. It told me you were the one. It's why I know you can do it." Then he smirked, "Plus, not being indebted to Cormac is a perk. I'll see you in fifty."

He stopped talking and I watched his body melt into the ground. It wasn't like watching him go into quick sand and he didn't puddle, it was like he was slowing being poured into thirsty soil that was greedy for water.

When he was no longer visible, I still waited another ten minutes before I began.

I was standing on a golf course that would have served the elite of Vegas only a few months ago and preparing to do a chant to protect a Ground Fae. Things just kept getting weirder and weirder.

Stepping into place, I took the knife out and ran it across my wrist. It might have been too deep but I didn't want to run out of blood halfway around the tree. I slowly chanted as I circled around, dribbling my blood. I took a final step and completed the circle and stepped back, waiting for something to happen, anything that would signal some magic had taken place.

After a few seconds, a dull light started to glow where I had stepped and then a mist, like the kind I had used, started to seep up from the ring I had created. This was good. Then the glow started to subside and the mist evaporated. Another couple of minutes and it would probably be safe to leave.

I'd preformed my first magic. Damn, I’d done well. Considering it was my first controlled use of magic, I was feeling pretty proud. The light continued to dull at the same rate and the mist was already gone. I'd be back at the casino in no time. It almost felt too easy.

A couple of rippers floated into the area. I wasn't surprised. They always found me if I stayed in one spot too long. They didn't scare me as much as they used to, but I wasn't thrilled they were here either.

"Hey, don't touch that!" I said when one of them ripper started looking at the still fading ring. It bowed its head and drifted off, like it understood me and I didn't even have mist seeping out of my mouth.

I kneeled down to look at the dull light that was getting dimmer and dimmer. As I got closer, I saw it start to surge brighter again. I wished I'd gotten better instructions. What if I'd messed it up?

I didn't know what happened next but I was thrown off my feet and flying through the air and hitting every branch on the way until I lost consciousness.

#

"Wrong? She wrong?" I awoke to a childlike voice.

I was lying on my stomach, my head bent to the right, and I felt like I'd just survived a nuclear blast.

"We lick?" a slightly lower voice asked.

Lick? I raised my right eyelid, my left too swollen to open, and saw two rabbits sniffing around my head. I couldn't see who had been talking. I closed the one eye and tried to assess the damage.

I couldn't take a deep breath, so I probably had a couple of cracked ribs. I tried to shift to my side and everything below my right thigh just flopped. Was I healing already? I didn't know. But there were two issues. If I healed wrong, I'd have a hell of a time getting back to the casino. And secondly, if magic had done this damage, would I even heal? It could be like the bullets.

"Lick?" the voice said again and I felt a wet tongue on my hand.

Opening my good eye, I saw one of the bunnies licking my hand. Then its head popped up, and that of its companion as well. They stood perfectly still for a moment before they ran.

I heard the rustling of someone approaching and tried to drag myself upward. Maybe I could pull myself behind a bush until I healed some more. I strained upward and barely made it an inch off the ground. Change of plans: playing dead it was.

There was the sound of someone walking near my head before I felt the hands gently feeling me up and down.

I opened myself up to get a sense of who or what was touching me and my eye snapped open. Maybe snapped wasn't the right term but I managed to open the good eye a slit.

Cormac was squatting down on his haunches in front of me, looking at my one good eye, then grimaced as he looked at the rest of me.

"That bad?" I asked.

"Bad, but you'll heal."

"How did you know I was here?"

"I told you that you couldn't leave," he joked in a soft voice. His eyes looked down toward my legs and I could see the concern. "I should probably set your leg."

"I know."

He paused and I wondered if he paused to give me time or him.

"It's going to hurt."

"I know," I responded, trying to lighten the subject. He seemed to have more trepidation than I did. "You know I can take it. I'm getting pretty good at this pain stuff."

"I guess that happens when you're constantly

breaking stuff."

"Ha ha ha. Just do it. I'm ready."

He nodded but didn't speak. He disappeared from my line of vision. He touched my legs and everything went black. I was glad. I didn't feel like screaming for the whole of Vegas to hear.

When I awoke next, I was cradled in Cormac's arms, being carried down the Vegas Strip.

"Why did he go under so early?" he asked.

"He just said he got called early. How'd you know?" I'd just done it.

"I saw the sealed ground," he explained.

"How did you find me out here? We're you following me?"

"I had things to take care of," he said.

"What stuff? Me?"

"Not everything has to do with you."

I gave up. He wasn't going to let me nail him down to an answer.

"What happened after you did it?"

"The light I think. The light *I* made. Is that normal? Did I trip some sort of magical alarm?"

"You're the maker. You can't trip it."

This was the first time we'd been together that hadn't been angry fighting or ignoring the other person. I wanted to lean my head back on his shoulder just be with him. I missed him. But he kicked me out and said we were done so instead of staying in his arms the way I wanted to, I said, "I can walk."

"Your knee was pretty bad," he said and kept

walking, and I didn't argue.

He stopped a few blocks away and dropped my legs to the ground. I instinctively put all my weight on the good leg.

"Can you walk?"

I tested my weight, taking a couple of steps with a slight limp. "Not perfect but I'll make it."

It was early morning hours so only the security detail was up and a couple stragglers when we walked in.

"Do you need help getting up to your room?" Cormac asked.

No, but can you come with me anyway, or better yet, take me home with you? "I'm fine. Thanks." I limped toward the stairwell and I didn't look back.

CHAPTER NINETEEN

Other than a slight stiffness from growing back new cartilage, my knee was almost perfect by the next morning as I observed the chaos on the seventh floor. I wasn't surprised that Burrom hadn't left anyone in charge. He'd think it was their problem to straighten things out after he was gone. I also remembered him talking about how people should find the natural leader among them, all others were doomed to fail anyway.

Nobody really took notice of me with all the chattering going on about where Burrom was, but I wasn't sure how long that would last. I was accepted here because of Burrom; now that he was gone, that could change quickly. My castle unit was a bit spooky but it was starting to grow on me.

I strolled down to the room where the Fae had a little restaurant area set up. They didn't like being forced to eat with other races and would dine here often. I poured myself a coffee from the large coffee urn on the table.

I took a sip and walked over to where the garbage was. When I'd returned last night, the full magnitude of my situation hit me. I was living in a place filled with enemies. I couldn't rely on Cormac. Even Burrom, who I never fully trusted, was gone. I didn't have the luxury of making any more mistakes.

I reached into my back pocket and grabbed my flask and threw it in the trash. It was time to grow up. That meant no more rash decisions and no more emotional crutches. It was one thing to have a drink but I couldn't afford to be fuzzy half the time.

I was turning to walk out when Buzz surprised me as he stepped into the room.

"Do you know where Cormac is?" Buzz asked in a nonchalant manner, contrasting the impression I had gotten from his rushed entrance.

It didn't make sense that he'd ask me where Cormac was. I knew he'd heard I'd moved out, or been kicked out if you wanted to get technical.

I shrugged. "How would I know? Maybe he's downstairs."

"Can you come with me?"

If it was going to be about Cormac, I didn't want to talk about it. He made his choice. Last night didn't change any of that. I wanted to say no, but Buzz looked so stressed out I didn't have the heart. I nodded, took my coffee and led him back to my room. One of the pluses of the castle room is the stone was real enough and thick enough to buffer out most noises and afforded a nice amount of privacy.

I opened the antique looking wooden door that stood out like a sore thumb in the hallway and welcomed him in.

"Have a seat," I said and motioned to the archaic looking velvet throne chair in the corner that had shown up a day after I'd moved in.

"Your room's a little scary."

"I know, but it grows on you," I said as I pulled out a stray feather that had already half escaped the feather mattress that was surprisingly comfortable. It made me wonder why we'd ever moved to springs. "Why are you all worked up?"

"The wolves are taking the humans' food rations in exchange for protection."

I leaned my forehead onto my palm. I'd suspected that was going on. It was hard not to hear the whispers but I was a lot happier before it had been laid at my feet.

"Protection from whom?" *Anybody but the wolves, please.* If I opened up that can of worms, it wouldn't be simply fixing a problem. I had too many raw nerves in that area and this was supposed to be my first day without booze?

I still hadn't decided what to do about the situation with my mother. The wolves had killed her. I'd decided to drink that thought away for a while but if I was going to be sober now there would be no buffer left to disguise that issue. At some point, I'd have to deal with it and I wasn't ready yet.

"The wolves."

"Does Cormac know about this?"

"I don't think he realizes how bad it's gotten."

Or thinks that the humans should handle some of their own problems, was more like it. I wished I could turn a blind eye but there were kids probably going hungry because of this. I knew what it was like to go hungry.

I'd decided to take my life into my own hands when I was thirteen. When you don't have a family calling the police and pressuring them to find you, it's not that hard to disappear. Laying low for a month was all it took to fall off the radar.

The idea of kids being extorted for their food and .... I wasn't going to think about what else.

"What about Vitor?" I asked. Vitor was my last ditch hope of staying out of this mess. Between the kids and my mother, the wolves were an emotional minefield.

"Have you seen Vitor lately?" Buzz asked.

Vitor was a walking disaster, and in a world full of people barely hanging on to their sanity, if you stood out as worse than the rest, you were a hair away from Bedlam.

I got to my feet and did a little hop, making sure my knee was in full working order first. Good as new.

"Where's Rogo?"

"He's on fourteen, holding court like usual. But you can't piss them off."

I walked to my old ancient door and held it open, waiting for Buzz. "You came here wanting help. I'm helping, but it's going to be done my way. Do you want me to do something or not?" I offered him a choice that didn't exist. I was going, with or without him.

"Maybe we should wait for Cormac?"

"You just said Cormac is missing. If I don't handle this now they'll think it's a free for all whenever Cormac is gone."

He started to follow me and I shut the door behind us.

"Should we get Dodd?" he asked.

"Nope," I said as we entered the busy stairwell. If magic was going to take the elevators, it should have at least added another staircase. The foot traffic could drive me back to drinking and I didn't even have my flask anymore.

"But what about the bad blood with you and them?"

"So you *did* think of that before dragging me into this. Thanks. And that's why we aren't getting Dodd. If we go to Rogo with a large entourage, it escalates it. It also makes him think I'm scared of him."

"He *is* a little rough around the edges."

"He's a show boater. I can handle him." I laid a hand on Buzz's arm. "Unless I'm on the verge of dying...don't step in. Just stand by me and look scary."

"I'm not sure I did the right thing," Buzz mumbled under his breath.

"Too late."

I needed to assert myself over these thugs if I wanted any chance of getting this under control. With them, you were either an alpha or you were stepped on. I couldn't turn to Cormac for every problem and I didn't know if I would ever leave this place. If I was going to stay, I was determined to be a force to be reckoned with.

I opened the door to the fourteenth floor. It was strange how each level, which used to be almost identical, now had its own flavor. Burrom's was mystical but slightly seedy, almost like how I would imagine an opium den.

Rogo's floor, on the other hand, was like stepping into a boxing club. Testosterone ruled this floor. It didn't matter how many women there were, it screamed boys' club. All the tank tops displaying bulging muscles pissed me off from the moment I hit the floor. Didn't any of them own a shirt with sleeves?

No one guarded the entrance because no one in his or her right mind would want to be here.

They all stared at Buzz and I, as we took a few steps into what they thought of as their domain. That was their first mistake. This place wasn't theirs. If they were a little smarter, they'd realize that most of the people here, unless you were a

Keeper, were tools to Cormac. They had no power, but that sort of thinking came down from the top.

Rogo thought their contribution made them special. They were as favored as the newest tool in the shed. And just like the tool, they would be used and abused and thrown to the curb when they had nothing left to give.

"I need Rogo," I demanded of the first group of guys I neared.

I got a couple sneers but one of them jerked his thumb toward the right. "Room sixty-nine."

I rolled my eyes. It was so easy I didn't bother commenting. My sarcastic mockery deserved loftier targets.

I walked past several open doors and tried not to look into any, no matter what odd noises I heard. I didn't want to see anything. I already had too many bad visions stored in my "I wish I hadn't seen that" mental album.

The door marked sixty-nine was closed when we got there and I rapped my knuckles on the surface.

When it cracked open, I recognized the face but couldn't recall the name.

"What do you want?" the goon asked.

I took a deep calming breath. Don't flip out, at least not yet. *You need to get in the room and near Rogo. No more stupid decisions that don't get you anywhere.* Buzz, on the other hand, was ready to lose his shit completely and he was supposed to be the calm one.

"I'd like to talk to Rogo."

His eyes slowly worked down the length of me. By time they hit my waist, I'd had enough. There was being tactical and there was being a disrespected schmuck. "Now."

A little of the mist seeped out of my mouth with the word. Anger. I had to remember the magic was linked to intense emotions. When I was upset around the humans, it might not be a good idea to speak. Right now, I was quite happy about it.

It didn't affect him like the rippers or make him do anything, but it scared him enough to back away from the door and let us in.

Not surprisingly, this was one of the suites as well, just as I'd expected. I looked around, eight men, four women. We were totally outnumbered. It was the story of my life. Why should this time be any different?

Rogo was reclined in the corner, a part of the group but somehow slightly removed.

"We need to talk," I said. There was a room off to the side. If he was going to play nice, he'd offer me privacy.

"Go ahead," he said.

He wasn't going to play nice. Fine by me. I felt many things about him, but nice wasn't on the list.

The jackass didn't even bother standing and he eyed me up like I was wearing a mini skirt and halter top instead of jeans and a long sleeve tee.

No problem. I walked over to him, stopping just within striking distance. If he caused a problem, I'd take the head off the snake.

"Stop scaring the humans and then taking their food for protection."

He snorted before he replied. "Why do you care about them? They hate your guts, or haven’t you noticed?" The room filled with laughter, everyone there knowing. It would be impossible not to. Living in this casino was like living in a small town with lots of little old ladies staring out their windows and gossiping every day.

"They hate us all," Buzz said. I cringed, knowing the opening he'd just handed him.

One, two, three...

"Not like her. They like anyone better than her."

There it was.

"I don't care who likes who. I'm telling you to stop it."

"Cormac's the big man." The way he said it wasn't flattering. "If he doesn’t like it, he can stop it."

"You don't understand. This isn't a debate."

Rogo finally decided to stand, thinking he could use his larger frame to intimidate me. If Cormac couldn't make that tactic work, Rogo had no shot. I felt Buzz move closer behind me but I threw him a look that told him he better stand down. I didn't want it to look like I needed protecting. I didn't.

Rogo, at his full height, towered over me. It gave him the wrong impression that he had a chance of taking me down. He didn't. What felt like ages ago, I'd taken his predecessor down a couple of pegs and I'd take him down just as easily.

He stepped in a little closer and I felt his hand cup my ass. I choked on my nausea as I let him pull me close to him.

"Why's a pretty little thing like you running around playing cop anyway? You should be with a real man who knows what a girl like you needs, a man who could protect you."

I laid a hand on his chest as if I were being compliant. Please, Buzz, just give me a minute. I turned my head down a moment, playing at being coy to buy time.

Sweat started accumulating on his brow and his shirt grew moist. I got a little nervous I'd given him a bit too much umph. I knew the gist of what I was doing, swelling the cells in his chest near his heart, making it harder for the blood to flow, but I didn't have any real practice. Up until now, I'd just thought of it in theory. If I actually killed the guy, it might not look too good. I stopped quickly, hoping it hadn't been too much.

He dropped his hands from me at almost the same time and tried to back away out of reach, but I just followed him backward.

"What's wrong, Rogo? You not feeling good? You look a little pale and sweaty." My voice was pitched higher than I normally talked.

He looked down at me, the light in his eyes going off. He tried to shove me away but I locked my free arm around him while I kept my other hand near his shoulder, not too far from his heart.

"What are you doing?"

"Nothing," I think. "I thought we were just getting familiar with each other. Now that we're all cozy, do I have your word you'll back off the humans, or do I have to get a little more personal, maybe a more permanent relationship, until you learn?"

"I'll stop," he whispered, barely getting the words past his lips.

"Somehow I knew you would." I let go and stepped back from Rogo. "Would anyone else care to get friendly?" I looked around the room, meeting each stare, assessing who had the balls to come for me at some later point. A slightly smaller wolf stood in the back of the room. He looked a little more scared than the others did. Petrified might have been a good description. I'd have to remember him and check into that.

"Let's go," I said to Buzz.

We walked from the room, wolves jumping out of the way to avoid me. The wolves in the hall had all planted themselves against the wall as we passed, proving they'd been eavesdropping.

"If Cormac hears about this, *when* Cormac hears about this, he's going to have my head on a fucking platter," Buzz groaned next to me as we entered the stairwell.

"Cormac doesn't own me and we aren't like that."

"I am soooo fucked," he continued, ignoring me as he banged his head against wall.

"Are you hearing me?"

"Yeah...I know. You're not Cormac's. You and Cormac are nothing. Uh huh," he said but then banged his head again. "The only people that believe that are you and Cormac."

I stopped and rested a hand on Buzz's shoulder and spoke in the nicest voice I could muster up after almost killing a man. "Can you stop banging your head before more people see you? It's not a good look."

Luckily, he turned around and started acting normal before we entered the lobby and saw Crash. He stood in front of the spot the elevators used to be, no longer dressed in fatigues and in the bright lights of the casino. A couple thoughts popped into my head, competing for attention. One, couldn't we dim these things? We didn't have this kind of fuel to be wasting. The second was I hadn't realized Crash was good looking.

He didn't smile, but the way he was eyeing me up, I could tell it was a mutual appreciation.

"I was looking for you," he said as we stepped into the lobby area.

"What can I do for you?" I asked, not slowing my stride as I headed through what used to be the casino gaming floor.

Crash fell into step alongside me and Buzz fell back but not out of sight.

"I don't know where Cormac is, but I'm going

back, with or without him. He can't just disappear and think we're going to wait. When we came back, the agreement was we would get reinforcements, not sit on our asses."

"It's barely been a day. He'll be here tonight." I hoped, because Crash wasn't going to be held off for long, and neither was I.

I eyed up the crowd as we walked. I was looking for wolves that seemed to be up to no good, but avoided any direct eye contact with the humans.

"Why do you walk through here when it makes you so uncomfortable?"

I stiffened. "I don't know what you're talking about."

"Oh...I think you do."

I stopped in the middle of what had become the town center of our little civilization with all eyes on me. They were always on me, haunting my every step. "You want to get all chummy? Fine, answer some of my questions."

"Some, not all." He looked around. It was obvious we were the center of attention. "Here?"

"No," I said and started walking again. "There's a place on the seventh. It's a nonhuman hang out that..."

"I've heard of it."

"You work quick."

"Have to."

"Be there at ten."

He walked away without answering.

"What are you doing?" Buzz asked as he came up next to me.

"Getting info."

"Seemed like he was looking to get more than that."

"Just because he looked at me? Don't worry about him. I can handle this."

CHAPTER TWENTY

This was the first time I'd come here since it had opened. It was Burrom's, or had been. He'd opened it a day or so after he had gotten settled, knowing instinctively that the Fae and wolves were going to need a place like this to blow off steam and try to feel normal. From what I'd heard, there was a similar place that catered to the humans somewhere on the main casino floor.

I got several looks as I walked into the place that used to house one of the many casino restaurants and I knew that I'd picked the right outfit. The small tight black dress hugged every curve I had, of which there were many.

I spotted Crash across the bar, hanging near a door that opened onto an abandoned balcony. It used to be the most packed area of the joint but the new view left a lot to be desired. When you were looking for escape, not reality, ruins could really dampen your mood.

His eyes roved over me as I approached, but not in a sleazy way. Just a man who knew his worth, letting a woman know he knew hers.

He wore a button down shirt and slacks, similar to what Cormac liked to wear and it made me sad. Crash was an attractive man, but he wasn't Cormac. The similarities in clothing just made me think of all the differences.

If Cormac were here, he wouldn't like this meeting even a little, but he was out doing his own thing, who knew where. I had to stop worrying about what Cormac liked. Fuck Cormac.

Crash smiled when I finally reached him. He straightened from where he'd been leaning against the doorframe and handed me one of the matching drinks he held.

I took the glass with no intention of drinking it and I nodded my head outside.

"You don't mind the rippers?" he asked.

There weren't any hovering nearby right now but that didn't mean they wouldn't show up at any moment. Even though they couldn't get that close to the casino, people tended to avoid the balcony because of the rippers as much as the ruins.

I shrugged, noncommittally, not sure if I should tell him I could make them heel, not that it mattered. I still hated the look of them and what they represented.

We walked over and I leaned on the balcony

railing.

"You first," I said.

"He's got my daughter, Maggie."

I was taken aback at his open omission. "I'm sorry," I said, knowing nothing would be adequate or make that feel any better.

He leaned next to me. "She's all I have left. She's what you people call the *changed*."

"So you joined him?"

He raised an eyebrow at me.

"I didn't mean it like that." I stared out at the ruins before I spoke again. "I get it. It's easy to be idealistic when you aren't the one making the choices. You sit back from your safe vantage point and say what should have been done. Then, one day, you're the one making the tough calls and you don't even know who you are anymore. You just keep wondering what happened, how you got there. And maybe the biggest question, how can you get the hell out of this."

"The closer I get to him, the closer I get to Maggie. Once I have her, I'll leave. There are settlements springing up in areas where the rippers don't like to go."

"Where is that?"

"Anything along the tornado wall. They hate being near it." He took a sip of what looked like scotch. "Your turn, why do you walk through the casino floors every day when you hate being there?"

"I used to stroll through the casino before

everything fell apart. I liked the energy, the activity. Now I guess I do it to hold on to some part of what I used to be. If I start hiding now..." I swirled the liquid around in the glass but I wouldn't drink it. "If I hide now, I might never show my face again. Sometimes I feel like I'm a hair's width away from breaking." I regretted the words the minute they left my mouth. This guy was working for the other team and I'm telling him how weak I feel. What was wrong with me?

"You underestimate yourself."

I turned to look at him, mere inches away from me.

"People like you don't break." His fingers glided across the skin of my cheekbone. "You're like forged steel; the wounds only make you stronger."

I looked into his warm hazel eyes. This man would never tell me to get out when he didn't get what he wanted. He wouldn't push me to my limits. Being with him would be easy and the invitation was clear. Only thing was...he wasn't Cormac. And oh yeah, he worked for the senator. Was I really this desperate for someone that I'd even consider him?

And then, for someone like me who tried to swallow back their feelings at every moment, I realized what I was doing. I missed Cormac, and I wanted to fill the gaping hole he'd left behind with anything I could find and stop the bleeding. I leaned against the railing, feeling more depressed than ever. All Crash did was make me want Cormac more.

I tensed suddenly when I saw Cormac through the opening of the balcony door. I didn't know that he ever came here or I never would have suggested the place. He'd probably heard I was here with Crash and wanted to know why I was fraternizing with the senator's man.

"You sure you know what you are doing with that one?" Crash asked. "And don't look at me like that. It's very obvious there's something going on between you two."

"I'm not doing anything with him."

"He's a hard man. He'll hurt you if you get in his way. You know that, don't you?"

I knew that better than anyone did. I wanted to deny it, say it wasn't true, but I couldn't. So I said nothing

"You really want him?" Crash asked.

"Yeah, I do."

He smirked and took a step closer.

"I'm going to do you a favor." Crash's hand curved around my back.

"He's not going to care for those reasons. He's done with me. He just wants to know what I'm doing out here with you."

"No one looks at a woman like that if he's done."

"This isn't a good idea."

We were alone on the balcony and I took a breath and looked over to where I knew Cormac was standing by the door. But he wasn't looking at me at all, he was looking down at a pretty little cocktail waitress.

"Humor me," he said.

Crash's hand pulled me the rest of the way into him and I let him. His lips feathered over mine in a teasing manner. He could be the best kisser in the world, but there was nothing Crash could have done that would've made me want him. There was no room left.

"Leave. Now." Cormac's voice was two feet away from us.

Crash opened his mouth to speak, took another look at Cormac and walked from the balcony. He looked back at me and winked right before he disappeared back into the bar.

He stared at me as if he wanted to kill me.

"The senator's man?" he didn't say anything else, just stared at me like I was beneath his contempt.

The spark of hope that this was jealousy crashed and burned. Yeah, getting hot and heavy with a guy that was with the senator wasn't the best move, but no one had seen me but Cormac. I was too hurt to care if it had been stupid. It was a kiss and now at least I had my answer. He didn't care.

"Yes, the senator's man. So what?" I knew it was a lame answer but I just didn't care right now. He was really through with me and the truth burned like a hole in my chest, making it hard to breathe.

"You're going to stand here and cavort with the enemy, in my casino?"

He took a couple of steps toward me and I didn't move an inch. His body radiated barely controlled rage and I didn't care. I just wanted something from him. Anything other than the cold disinterested looks I'd started to expect.

"Sorry, I'll make sure to leave your casino when I sleep with him. It's just that we currently have a lack of hotels in business, and well, I'm sure you get the..." the words died as I watched his control start to slip. Oops, I might have taken it a little too far this time I thought as I belatedly realized that even Cormac had a limit, and I think I'd just hit it.

His hand wrapped around my wrist and he pulled me along after him through the bar. A path opened up in front of us as anyone who looked at him for even a second skirted out of his way. Everyone watched us pass by and I thought I heard someone say, "Is he going to kill her?"

He dragged me after him into the stairwell and I tried to yank back control of my arm.

"Let me go," I yelled.

He ignored me and kept walking.

He didn't release me until we walked into the living room of the penthouse.

Dodd and Buzz were on the couch when we walked in.

"Get out," Cormac said, but it was

unnecessary. They took one look at him with me trailing behind and they were already scrambling to leave.

I watched him stalk across the living room floor and I wondered how long it was going to take before he spoke. I didn't have to wait more than a few seconds. The moment the door clicked shut behind Buzz and Dodd, he exploded.

He turned to me, with anger pouring out of him. "I guess you don't care where you get it now?"

The words felt like a blow and for the first time, I didn't want to yell. I didn't have it in me to fight with him anymore. If this was what he thought of me, it was over anyway. There was no point.

"He's not the senator's man." My voice was flat and emotionless.

"Forget it." He shook his head and walked away from me. "You want to sleep with him, then go do it. Sleep with all of them. You can leave with them too." He moved around the room and grabbed some papers off the table, ignoring me already.

I should leave. He told me to get out. I'd leave soon.

"And stop doing that," he said when he looked up at me and I was still in the exact same place.

"Doing what?"

"Looking at me like that. Like I rejected you." The anger was seeping back.

"Haven't you?"

"I would've given you everything I had and you didn't want it." He turned away from me and walked to the bar.

I had no argument. What was there for me to say? I only *temporarily* rejected you? I didn't want everything but hey, I was willing to sleep with you?

"Get out," he said again, not looking at me any longer.

He was so angry. Maybe he had never stopped being angry. I could see it in his every movement. Self-preservation told me to leave. I wasn't built for a relationship, my childhood had beat that out of me, and a life with him would never be easy.

So why wouldn't my legs move? Why did I have this overwhelming fear that if I left this time, it would be different, final? That if I ran from him this time, he'd just let me disappear.

"No." It wasn't an eloquent expression of love but I thought it got my point across. I hoped it did because I was having a hard enough time standing my ground.

I watched as he poured himself a drink. A vein pulsed in his neck. He threw back a glass and then another.

"I'm done with the cat and mouse game." He looked at me, letting me see what he was thinking. He still wanted me and with an intensity that scared me to my core.

It was a final warning.

And I still didn't move. I'd rather brave the storm than lose him.

Our eyes met and held. He put his glass down on the bar in a slow and deliberate motion and started walking toward me.

Five steps away, four, three...

He paused a mere inch from me.

"Last. Chance."

My mouth grew dry. I didn't say a word, just stood there. I was scared of what being with him would mean but more terrified of not having him at all.

He was so close but not touching me. His silver-grey eyes roved up and down my body as if I were a feast he was about to devour and a chill rushed through me. He laid his hands in unison on my waist and then slowly guided them upward, until they brushed the underside of my breasts, before they moved downward again. I was embarrassed because he'd barely touched me and my breathing was already heavy and my heart was beating rapidly in my chest. He didn't seem to notice or care.

His hands drifted lower, following the contour of my hips and then lower until they reached the hem of my dress. His fingers gripped it, sliding his hands back upward, with the dress in tow, until it bunched around my waist.

His hands reached around and cupped my ass, pulling me up on my tiptoes until I was flush against his erection.

"Do you think..."

"Shut up." His lips covered mine in an

onslaught that made me forget what I even wanted to say. I was drowning in sensations. A small part of me poked its head up and said he was overwhelming me on purpose. The other ninety-five percent was drowning in him and didn't care. He ground against me and the last coherent part of my brain shut down.

I didn't even know we had moved about the room until I felt a cool surface of the bar underneath me and my hips were teetering on the edge, the pressure of Cormac against me, in between my legs, keeping me in place.

He pulled my dress over my head and pressed me back against its surface. Laying there only in a thong, his eyes roved over me and I started to grow self-conscious.

"No," he said pulling my arms to my side. "You don't get to hide after how long you've made me wait." His hands replaced mine as they cupped my breasts, taking one nipple into his mouth, then the other, until they were hard buds.

He leaned back, still looking at me as he started to unbutton his shirt. He had the most glorious body I'd ever seen, all dark tanned muscles.

Once his shirt was removed, he undid his pants and shed everything in one swoop. His large penis jutted out and panic shot through me as he stepped back in between my thighs.

As if he knew I was starting to panic, his hand reached in between us, one finger entering me as another rubbed between my folds. I heard myself moan as if I were a different person and I couldn't catch my breath. I felt him remove his fingers as something much larger pushed for entry, as his other hand never stopped rubbing my flesh. My legs wrapped around him, wanting more as my back arched.

He plunged all the way into me with one thrust, and then he paused. His face close to mine, he watched me.

When I nodded that I was okay, he withdrew slowly and thrust back in. His hands cupped my breasts before they moved into my hair, cupping my head and angling it as his lips moved over mine. His tongue delved into my mouth at the same time as his hips pressed into mine.

I threw my head back as the pace quickly became frantic and overwhelming. My legs pulled him deeper as the intensity of the sensations grew. His hands gripped my shoulders, pulling me firmly to him, as I exploded. A last final thrust had him roaring over me.

I would've laid there indefinitely in my languor, without the smallest inclination to move, but Cormac had other ideas. Without withdrawing himself, he wrapped his arm around my hips and lifted me off the bar with him. He walked us both into his room. I fell backward onto his bed with him following me down.

"What are we doing?"

"You didn't think that was it, did you?" he

asked. "I'm going to fuck you so well, that the next time you leave this room, there won't be any doubt left in your brain that you're mine."

CHAPTER TWENTY-ONE

I learned last night that Cormac didn't believe in a learning curve. It didn't matter. I hadn't wanted one. After waiting all this time, I wasn't looking for the b version. Cormac got under my skin in a way I couldn't explain.

He'd been gone when I woke in his large bed this morning. I was convinced he wasn't sleeping anymore. Something was going on with him, but I didn't know what; all I did know was that a normal man couldn't have done what he did last night.

When the devil himself walked into the living room, part of me wanted to freeze in a panic, now that the flesh of my memories stood before me. The "lusty me" of last night knew exactly how to act. That Jo wanted to jump all over him and go another few rounds. The "slightly awkward morning me" opted for casual nonchalance.

"What's different about you?" It wasn't the first words I thought I would be saying to him but it certainly broke the ice.

"I thought that was supposed to be my line."

"You aren't sleeping anymore and I thought men couldn't do it that many times in a row," I continued, blowing my laid back "I'm above it all" persona. I didn't sweat it too much. I would've blown that soon enough anyway. I was more of an in the trenches, getting dirty type.

"Everybody is going to be here soon," he said, changing the subject.

"I know. Got the memo." It had been lying next to my pillow. Some people woke to roses after a night of sex, I woke to war meeting details.

"I brought up a few of your things. They're on the top shelf of the closet," he said as he headed out of the room.

I grabbed the cover off the bed and walked into the closet and saw the stack of my stuff. I guess no one ever explained to Cormac a few meant three. *Don't freak, it's just some stuff.*

I should have expected this. My actions last night, especially the ones that had coincided with lots of groaning, pretty much declared I was all in. I wanted Cormac, and I didn't want him with anyone else. Even the idea made me want to kill someone.

I tugged on jeans I didn't remember owning and a snug v-neck tee as I took another calming breath. This was the end of the world. Why sweat a long-term relationship if I might not live another week? I decided to look on the bright side: if I died tomorrow, one day did not a relationship make. And, in the meantime, I needed to get as much sex as I could before I died. Lots of hot sex was currently number one on my bucket list.

I cleaned myself up and headed into the living room, just as Dark walked in carrying a couple of boxes stacked on top of each other.

"Where do you want them?" he asked Cormac.

"My room, thanks."

"Gotchya. Dodd is a couple seconds behind me with the rest," Dark said.

"What's in them?" I asked Dark as he was walking past me.

"Your stuff," he said with a smile, apparently happy about our change in situation.

I took another deep breath. It's okay. I could be dead tomorrow.

I took a few steps closer to Cormac and said in a hushed voice, "I'm not saying I have a problem with it, but don't you think you should've told me before you had my stuff moved?"

"Why?" He reached down and popped a grape into his mouth from the bowl on the table.

"Where did we get grapes?" I asked, fresh fruit making all other subjects pale in comparison. I greedily grabbed one. My mouth watered like crazy, as I bit down on the juicy sweetness. I missed fresh fruit more than most things. All the produce in the casino and the immediate area had gone rotten.

"Now that we know which people won't get eaten they were able to scout out a bigger distance. They brought them back this morning," Cormac explained. "And while we're on the subject of food, stop giving yours away."

He eyed me up as if he already knew all the details but I played stupid anyway. "Huh?" I said as I popped a couple of grapes quickly in my mouth so I didn't have to talk.

"I know you've been sneaking some of yours to the kids," he stood there and waited for me to finish chewing.

"Do you have my every move watched?"

"This is my casino...castle, or whatever it is now. I know everything that happens here. And I mean *everything*." He stopped to pop another grape in his mouth and I digested what that meant.

I looked at him, trying to gauge if he really did, but didn't comment.

"And everyone is getting plenty to eat. Stop giving yours away. We aren't indestructible. You still need food and you're getting too thin." He ran a hand over the side of my waist. He pounded on my back when I nearly choked on my grape.

I'd seen people act like this. This was normal couple behavior. I am officially part of a couple now.

I caught the look on Cormac's face. "Why are you smirking?"

"Because I know what you're thinking."

"No you don't." I pushed the hair from my

face.

"Oh, yes I do."

He lifted a stem with a single grape hanging from it and brought it to my mouth. Instead of taking it with my mouth, I plucked the grape with my fingers. "Fine. Maybe you do."

I chewed on it while he laughed.

"And you're not as funny as you think you are," I said once I finished.

"Don't be upset, snookums."

I didn't respond as I heard the door open and Rogo walked in the room. He greeted us both but only looked my way for a fraction of a second. It was enough to see the hatred.

He was still pissed off about me showing him up at his place. I waited for Cormac's reaction. If he knew what had gone down, he wasn't saying, but that didn't mean anything.

Dodd and Buzz came in shortly after carrying what appeared to be some more of my stuff that they deposited in the corner. Vitor came in next. Kirk, the Fae that was filling the vacuum created by Burrom's disappearance, showed up too.

I was surprised when Adam, spokesperson for the humans, showed up with Colleen in tow. From the glances they got, I wasn't the only one. How had Adam even known about the meeting? I didn't think anyone ever put him on the need to know list.

Dark came back in as everyone was getting settled.

The reaction to Crash's arrival was the strongest. He came alone, which showed balls. I was the only person in the room who wasn't shooting him daggers with their eyes.

"I'd like the floor for a minute," Adam said, drawing the attention back to him, the second least appreciated man in the room. No one spoke. That was about as much encouragement as you were going to get with this crowd.

"We know about the meetings."

"Really? You do? I thought it was just a stroke of luck you were here right now," Rogo said, laying on the sarcasm.

My inner wiseass wanted to laugh, but I wouldn't let it. I refused to laugh at anything Rogo said. I'd laugh at him, but not with him. I also felt bad for Colleen who, no matter how she tried to fake it, was visibly nervous.

"Let him talk," I said, looking for an excuse to antagonize Rogo.

Rogo looked at me, then around the room, snorted and nodded his head. He didn't need to say a word, it was clear as day to everyone in the room what he was implying. I needed the guys to back me or I'd be easy pickings. It was a complete lie and he knew it.

A smarter person would have let him save face. I'd emotionally castrated his ego the other day. Just for relations, I should let his pride have this salve. Then I saw Cormac's face and decided it would be better if I put him in his place than have

Cormac kill him. Rogo did have his uses.

I walked closer to him. "Get up."

"Why? So your goons can jump me?"

"No, this stays between us. I don't need them to take you on and we both know it."

He didn't stand. "I don't fight girls," he said and swallowed hard.

"Coward." I walked away, not wanting the close proximity.

"Adam?" I said, handing him the floor.

"We want an equal say, a *real* say, in what goes down from now on," he said with a slight tremble in his voice.

Silence reigned for a few seconds while everyone digested this new slice of information, then the cacophony roared.

Rogo screamed something about them going back to huddling in the corners. Burrom's replacement, Kirk, yelled that they ate up the resources everyone else brought in. Cormac started explaining in his slightly condescending tone that he was generous enough to allow them to stay...but. Even Vitor got into the action, looking more alive than I'd seen him in weeks, declaring how they took up too much room in the casino.

It boiled down to the same question, "Why did they deserve input?" The consensus was that the humans had become the leeches of civilization.

A crack filled the air with a flash of light and brought silence again. Colleen, with her vivid purple eyes stood there, hand raised and her fingers smoking. The humans had discovered they had a trump card, the *changed*, and it looked like they were ready to play it.

"What was that?" I asked, figuring they'd have the least hostility toward me, at least in this moment. I was the only one who hadn't been shouting down their rights the minute they walked in the door.

"It's my lightning." Her voice was loud but I knew a false bravado when I heard it. She was nervous to be here but she came anyway and Colleen leaped in my esteem. "I've been practicing," she continued.

"I say that buys them a vote." I raised my hand and looked around the room. "Come on, she just shot lightning into the air. Controlled lightning, I might add, since the place isn't burning up right now."

I looked at Cormac for back up. He was leaning a hip against the bar and shrugged in an "I don't care either way" manner.

Nice back up, buddy. I should've written a contract up before we slept together so he understood exactly what it entailed outside the bedroom. It meant you have to agree with everything I say, especially when people I don't like are present. He was going to need some work at this relationship stuff too.

"What about the rest of the *changed*? Can they do shit like this?" Rogo asked, a bit less abrasive.

No, it wasn't just not abrasive, there was a tone to it that I couldn't place. Then I saw how Colleen looked at him. *Oh, hell no!* Rogo wasn't a bad looking guy but it was hard for me to admit it because he made my skin crawl. Colleen was noticing though.

"Yes, they can, on differing levels," I said and moved into a closer position to Colleen, while simultaneously throwing Rogo a dirty look.

"I vote yes," Rogo said, ignoring my dirty looks.

"Yes," Dark said from the corner, where he was being suspiciously quiet.

Cormac shrugged again and everyone else looked like they were prepared to accept the new situation.

"Now that your internal matters are under control, can we move on to the other issue at hand?" Crash said.

Cormac stepped forward. "Buzz?"

Buzz moved to the table and laid a large sheet of what looked like architectural plans on the table.

"We managed to find these where the company that owned the plant used to have offices," Cormac explained. "We've got to assume that however many Colleen saw and what we viewed that night is only a fraction of what is really there."

"So we use stealth," I said and looked up from the plans.

"Yes," Cormac said.

"Agreed," Crash said.

"We get our people out, then we go back and obliterate them." I felt his hand on my shoulder and I saw him look directly at Crash. "They knew they were taking something that was mine. People don't cross me and get away with it."

"If we come at them from the southeast, we'll get a better advantage I think," I said trying to move the topic along from Cormac's cave man claiming of me.

Cormac moved into a different war mode and switched gears. "There were three lookouts on the tops of these towers." He leaned over where I stood to point to the locations on the plans. Feeling him behind me made it hard to concentrate and I could've sworn he was messing with me.

"We get snipers to take those out simultaneously. My best guess is that they'll be holding our people in the most inner building, the one surrounded by the rippers."

"I'll handle the rippers," I said. The entire room stared at me, except Cormac.

"They're controlling them. Are you sure you can handle it?" Crash asked.

"Yes." No, not really, but I had the best shot.

"Jo," Crash said, "there were more than fifty of them in this area." He pointed to another building. "And there might have been even more behind here. How are you going to possibly keep them contained?"

No one spoke; I'm sure they were waiting for me to explain. Anyone that hadn't seen me keep them at bay by this point had still heard the whispers that I had some sort of strange connection with them, everyone but Crash, that is.

"I've got it. I'll take one other with me, but I can handle this," I reaffirmed. I looked to the rest of the group, wondering if I was going to experience any more opposition, but no one looked directly at me, not even Rogo.

"What is going on here?" Crash asked.

"Leave it alone," Cormac said.

"You're going to let her go in there alone?"

"If she says she can handle this, I believe her."

"What is wrong with you people? Especially you! No one can handle that many rippers."

"I said to drop it."

Crash just shook his head in disgust. He thought they were feeding me to the lions as a diversion. He didn't get it, I was the lion. It's why when the subject came up, no one wanted to look at me. They'd prefer to pretend whatever I had going on didn't exist. If they acknowledged it, they might not be able to walk the halls of this place with me.

"We need Katie." I looked at Adam, to see how willing he was going to be to offer up his people. "You're either on the team or you're not. There's no half measures," I said when he took a minute too long to reply.

"I'll ask her. Ultimately, it's her call."

"Agreed," I said.

"I'm going," Colleen said. "Don't even think to

argue. I can take down a man three times my size with no noise. Well unless they scream."

To know that, she's had some practice. I wanted to laugh but didn't want to steal her thunder.

"How is that possible?" Dodd asked.

"She uses it like a taser gun," I said, guessing. Colleen's smile confirmed I was correct.

"I'm more than willing to offer a demo," she said, looking around the room.

Not surprisingly, no one accepted to be the crash test dummy.

"I'm in," Dark said.

"Are your guys any good with a sniper?" Cormac asked Crash.

"Half my men were Green Berets before this. They're good at everything."

"You and your guys will hang back over here and take out the watchmen. Jo, who do you want to take with you to handle the rippers?"

"I'll take Colleen." I knew bullets wouldn't take out a ripper but Colleen's lightning might work.

"Done. You two keep the rippers in check. If our people aren't in this building, it could be any of these. I'll take this one with Katie, as long as she agrees. We still need more bodies. I want Dark to take this one with somebody and then we need people to cover this one."

"I'll cover one of them," Rogo said.

"Really?" Dark asked.

"Yes," Rogo snapped.

What's this guy's angle? Was it Colleen? Did he think if he could manipulate her and gain some control of the *changed*? Could we even trust him? And the most important question, did it matter? We didn't have the luxury of turning anyone down. He was among the wolves that the rippers wouldn't bother. It wasn't just about getting our people back, it was also about keeping everyone alive.

"We're still short two. And no," Cormac said as Dodd was about to argue why he should be going. "I'm sorry; Dodd, but you'd be a liability."

"Vitor? Kirk?" I asked, looking at both factions of the Fae.

"With all due respect," Kirk said, "this isn't our fight."

"You guys make me ashamed of my heritage," I said to the two of them.

"They aren't wrong," Cormac said. "It's not."

"What about the fact that they live here?"

"And they carry their weight."

I knew the Fae worked daily at reinforcing the wards around the Lacard, but the fact that they never put any skin in the game was getting old.

"They're our people. I'll get the two we're short," Adam said.

"Make sure they understand all the details," I stressed. "Make sure they know they might not be coming back."

CHAPTER TWENTY-TWO

There she was. I'd been searching for Katie for over an hour.

"Katie," I yelled when I saw her blond head bopping around. She turned and smiled when she saw me running down the hall of the main floor of the casino to catch up to her.

"I'm in," she said as I neared, still smiling. "Do you know when we're leaving?"

"Not yet. Colleen and Adam are getting more recruits." I looked at her and couldn't help but be jealous at the way, even after everything that had happened, she could still smile and seem happy. How could anyone roll with these kinds of punches and still smile all the time? I looked at her a little closer and thought maybe she was just crazy. Yeah, that made more sense. Nobody in their right mind could be this happy, with everything that was happening.

"I'm not actually here for that," I explained.

"Oh? What's up?"

I paused for a minute, embarrassed at the question I was about to ask. "You said there was a seer in the Lacard. Do you know where I could find her?"

"Yeah, usually she's on the main floor but I haven't seen her down here today. I'd try her room. She's in four twenty-two."

"Thanks." I smiled back at her even though I wanted to grimace. She was located in the heart of the humans, and not even the *changed*, who didn't harbor the same animosity towards me, but plain old Mary Jane and Dick. Oh well, it is what it is.

I took the stairs up to the fourth floor, put my hand on the doorknob and tried to settle my nerves. It was the middle of the afternoon, so it shouldn't be too crazy, with most people doing their socializing and duties elsewhere. That was just an assumption, because I hadn't been to this floor once since before the shattering.

Like I'd expected, there weren't too many people out and about. A group of teens loitered at the end of the hall and a few adults walked from one room to the next. It was a good thing because they all stopped and stared in my direction. Their faces all displayed the same sentiment. *What the fuck do you think you're doing here?*

I did the same thing I did downstairs. I lifted my chin and replied in a physical demeanor that said "I'm here and I don't give a shit if you like it or not." It was the farthest thing from the truth, but they'd never know that.

I walked down the hallway, getting closer and closer to the group of teens. Still so young and stupid, they were more of a problem than the adults, who actually thought of the consequences of their actions.

The six of them, four boys and two girls, spread out now and actually blocked the hallway. The adults suddenly disappeared into their rooms, not wanting to stop the trouble but making sure they didn't witness anything that could get them booted from the safety of the casino.

Dumb kids, didn't they listen to the gossip? I might take a couple of hits but they would be the ones recouping for weeks. Me getting hurt wasn't my fear. What if I accidentally killed one of them?

"You don't want to do this," I said when I was close enough for them to hear me in a quiet voice.

"She's scared," the largest boy said and they all started to laugh.

"Yes, I am. But not for me." I saw a flicker of panic run through their eyes and hope sprung up in me. Then one of the girls stepped forward.

"You think you're so hot because your Cormac's whore, but you're nothing. I could have him in a heartbeat but I wouldn't debase myself with a nonhuman."

Oh, silly little girl, Cormac would eat you for breakfast.

Wait, even the kids knew I'd slept with him already? The casino was becoming small town gossip purgatory.

"Let her through," an adult female voice said.

I looked down the hallway and there stood a woman with a turban wrapped around her head and a flowing floral print dress. Bingo. I'd found the seer.

The kids disbanded quickly, running down the hall in the opposite direction to the woman. The way they took off made me want to join them. These kids weren't scared of anybody. What freaked them out so badly about this woman?

"Come," she said. She turned and walked back down the hallway, her curvaceous figure sashaying as she moved. She disappeared into a room on the right.

I was too intrigued to leave, so I followed. This was what I came for, after all. I followed her into the room and she closed the door that I would've left open.

"I've been waiting for you," she said. "I'm Liza."

"You knew I was coming?"

"Still skeptical after everything that has happened. I'm not surprised. You're stubborn to the core." She sat down at the table in the corner. It had a colorful fabric thrown over it but I guessed it was the standard hotel table underneath. "Sit down." She pointed to the chair opposite her.

I settled in with nothing to lose now.

"Why did you come, if you don't believe?"

"I don't *not* believe."

"You are here for a reading, correct?" She lit the few candles in between us.

"It depends on the cost."

"Normally, it would be two days' rations, but for you this is free."

Two days' rations were steep for most people. I couldn't believe she was able to con them out of so much or perhaps that was just my price.

"I don't want free. If you're legit, I'll pay you." I didn't want to be indebted to anyone and certainly not a con artist.

"If you insist. Don't be alarmed."

She started to unwrap the turban on her head.

"Nothing you say will alarm me." This woman was seriously overestimated her spookiness. She was probably used to scaring all the little teens in the hallway. She didn't know what I'd seen in my life.

I looked out the window, wondering how long it was going to take this woman to finish grooming herself and get started. I had plenty of other things I wanted to do today.

"That's not why I warned you," Liza said. I turned back toward her, wondering if she was ready to get this sideshow going.

I caught myself from screaming but I didn't manage to stop myself from falling off my chair. There was an eyeball in the middle of her freaking forehead! Her black hair only accentuated the black colored eye even more, like it needed it. It was about the same size as her normal brown eyes, but darker with the pupil and iris indistinguishable from each other. It had eyelashes, but thankfully, no eyebrow. That might have pushed me over the edge.

"I warned you," she said, in a "told you so" manner.

"Was that always there?" I asked as I climbed back into my chair feeling like an utter fool. As soon as I thought I'd seen it all, the world knocked me right back on my ass. At some point, you would think I'd stop acting jaded and just relent to the truth: I didn't know anything.

"No, it grew in after the change. I thought it was a huge pimple at first." She laughed at her own joke, while I cringed.

"Were you always in this line of business?"

She reached over to her side and took out a deck of cards, wrapped in black silk. "Shuffle these," she said as she handed me the deck. "I used to tell fortunes on the strip. It's a family... used to be a family business. We've always had the knack of reading people. Then the change came. Now I can't shut it off." She pointed toward the cards. "Split the deck into three, using your left hand, and then restack them."

I placed the pile in front of her and she took the deck in her hands and simply held them, then closed her normal eyes, leaving just the single black one peering at me. I wanted to duck out of the room, but I managed to stay in the chair, even if I couldn't quite hold her one-eyed gaze.

"Aren't you going to lay them out or something?"

"You're concerned your friend, the doctor, is already dead but she isn't."

Everyone knew about Sabrina. "Will she be alive when I get there?"

"Yes, I think so."

"You aren't sure?"

"It's fuzzy, I can't say. I just know she's alive." She reached her hand across the table palm up.

Oh no, she wanted to hold my hand while her crazy eye stared at me. "Aren't you going to read the cards?"

"No, I don't think so. I'd rather feel your energy."

I eyed her palm, searching it for anything strange. It looked normal, no extra eyeballs or fingers.

"Your left," she instructed when I would've given her my right hand. Her normal eyes remained closed as the third eye stared at me.

I placed my left hand on hers.

"You're going to feel forced to make a choice between what looks like two bad options. You're going to make the wrong one."

"Can you get a bit more specific? Bad or worse have been my life. It's not really in the major revelation column."

Her normal eyes snapped open. "I can't be more specific. It doesn’t work like that. I just see you at a junction with dark paths in every direction."

"I need details."

"I doesn't show anything more."

I pulled my hand back from hers and stood up. "I think this might have been a waste of time."

She didn't argue, just shook her head as she watched me walk from the room. It wasn't until I was halfway out the door that she spoke. "When the war comes, you won't be able to fight it alone."

"What war?" I said, frozen.

"The one that's coming."

This woman was useless. "Oh, and I'm not alone, not anymore," I shot back as I left, not wanting to hear anything else from her. She probably just made everything up anyway. It didn't take a fortune teller to hear the rumors running around about the senator. Everyone was scared on some level that there would eventually be a war.

CHAPTER TWENTY-THREE

I'd just made it past the fourteenth floor, also known as the werewolf den, when I saw him heading down the stairs in the opposite direction of my climb. He was the wolf I had seen in Rogo's room the other day, the one that had been exuding fear.

He looked like he was in his mid-twenties, with lean muscles that hadn't filled out yet. Scraggly light brown hair hung in front of a smooth skinned face.

"Hi," I said as he got closer and tried to smile the way Lacey used to, back before everything had fallen apart. I shoved her memory away, not wanting to think about what might have become of her. "I'm Jo."

"Yeah, I know." He gave me a wide berth as he tried to move past me.

"Wait, where are you going?" I asked, reaching for his arm and forcing my face to keep its smile. *And what do you know about my mother, you dirt bag? Is that why you're so scared?*

He pulled out of my reach quickly, "Sorry, I've really got to get going."

"Jo?"

I turned to see a winded Colleen on the landing behind me, and I heard the young werewolf sprint away.

"What's wrong?"

"I've got two volunteers in addition to Katie. I thought you might want to approve them first. You know, before I brought them to the rest of the group."

I wanted to ask why she wanted my approval but I shut my mouth quickly. She was a young girl, obviously sensitive and insecure. I didn't know why, but I had a feeling she was trying to establish a relationship between us. She was the same girl that had shot daggers at me with her eyes not that long ago, but it was there in her stance, the way she was shifting her weight uneasily, eager for my approval.

"Do you think they are right for the job?" I asked.

"They were the first two I approached. They're both capable of handling themselves. Evan has great night vision and a wicked set of claws. Sharon's hard to explain. The closest description I can think of is a ninja."

"I think I remember Evan," or his claws,

anyway. "I don't remember seeing the name Sharon on the lists."

Colleen kicked at the stair in front of her with restless energy. "Uh, yeah. She's probably not on the list."

"If you think they're good, I'm good." And I wasn't saying it to just make her feel good. I found I did trust her opinion.

"Should we bring them by to meet everyone else?"

"Yes, we'll need to walk them through the plan."

"They're in? That's it?"

"Yes. I'll make sure it's fine. If you tell me that they're good, I believe you. Want to get a bite to eat with me?"

She jerked her eyes toward me, and away quickly, but followed me as I started to climb the stairwell again.

We climbed the stairs without speaking. Silence was the new polite thing to do. You didn't ask people about their family anymore because most of them were dead. You didn't ask kids about school, there was none. Summer plans? That was easy because it was the same for everyone...stay alive.

Colleen was in good shape and kept pace with me as I started taking the stairs two at a time.

"Why don't you take the elevator that's still left on the other side?" she asked.

"I like the physical exertion."

"Are you afraid of getting stuck?"

I laughed. "That too, but don't tell anyone."

"It's okay, I don't do it either. When the last ones disappeared, I could hear the crying from the people stuck in the stone. It was really horrible."

"I agree completely."

I looked at Colleen and I could see the idea come into her head the same time it did mine. "Count of three?"

"No one ever beats me," she replied.

"Til now...one, two...hey! You cheated!" I yelled after her laughing.

We made it to the penthouse in record time as we pushed through the door, both of us laughing. It didn't last long. Cormac, Rogo and Crash were there and it was back to the grind.

All three men's stares swung to us as we walked into the room.

"We've got three more," I said. "We're ready."

"They're good?" Cormac asked.

"Yes. They're good," I said, vouching for Colleen's choices.

"Okay. We call everyone in, go over the details and it's a go."

Crash made his goodbyes while keeping a distance from me, which wasn't surprising the way Cormac eyed his every step. Rogo left right after and Colleen would've walked out too, if I hadn't grabbed her arm. I didn't like the way Rogo was eyeing her up, yet again. It made my skin crawl.

I waited until it was just Cormac, Colleen and I

left in the room.

"I think you should stay with one of us until after we do the raid."

Cormac turned so he had his back to Colleen shot me a stare that said over his dead body.

I threw him back a look. *I get it but I don't trust Rogo.*

Cormac pulled out his funny phone. "I need you two up here," he said and hung up the phone and turned to Colleen.

"Are you sure?" Colleen asked, her eyes lighting up but weary as if we'd say we were kidding.

"Yes, positive," I said.

Dodd and Dark came in a minute later.

"What's wrong?" Dodd asked.

"Colleen's going to stay with you guys," Cormac said.

The confusion on their faces made it hard not to laugh, as they both looked at the empty extra bedroom, then each other and back to Cormac.

"Uh..." Dark said, clearly confused.

Dodd was going to be more of an issue but Cormac quickly quashed it with his next words. "We're all going to need a good rest before we go get Sabrina. I'm sure one of you guys won't mind taking the couch."

Dodd looked like he was sucking on a lemon as he nodded. "Sure."

"Good. Go help her collect her stuff," Cormac said as he ushered them out and locked the door behind them.

Finally alone, I walked back into the living room.

"What's the deal?" he asked, as he followed behind me and his hands circled my waist. He leaned his head down and nipped at my shoulder.

I leaned my head to the side to give him better access. "I don't like the way Rogo is looking at her. Besides, she's all alone."

"A lot of people are."

He was right. I couldn't walk down the hall without seeing kids with no one. Colleen had it better than most, because at least she could protect herself. "I don't know. There's something about her."

"She reminds you of yourself," he said as he steered me toward the bedroom.

"Why would you say that?"

"Because she might be the only person I've seen that is just as fucked up as you were."

"Do you think Dodd is really mad?"

"Not mad, just annoyed."

"Will he let her stay for a while?" I asked.

"If I make him, he will, but it's going to cost you," he said and covered my mouth with his as he pulled me onto the bed.

CHAPTER TWENTY-FOUR

It was eleven p.m. the next evening when we got to the place where Crash and his men had stashed their Hummers. The plan was to get there under the cover of night. The roads in this section of Vegas were next to impassable with all the debris. We had covered them with whatever we could find before we'd left them there, right outside the city. The roads in the suburbs were easier to travel because the buildings were smaller and more spread out. When a house collapsed, for the most part, it stayed on its own lawn. A couple of the town roads were harder because the commercial buildings didn't have lawns so their debris would fall into the avenues. They'd traveled the longer way around back to the casino with us. They hadn't felt comfortable leaving their trucks at the casino, near so many people that hated the senator.

I was relieved to see that the Hummers were still there. I was even more relieved when they started, proving their gas hadn't been siphoned out. I knew there were people that had survived the rippers, still hiding out in the ruins and scavenging. People that shunned living with anything magical, even if it meant eventual death.

We squeezed into the Hummers and it took us a while to loop around to the east of the compound, about five miles out. If things ever became normal again, I was so getting one of these trucks. They were badass and climbed over most of the things in their path.

We wound our way through the desert and stopped in a different spot than last time. They could've discovered our tracks and now be on the lookout for a group coming from that direction.

The snipers were going to be the hardest part of the plan. They were fully human and susceptible to rippers, but they had also assured us that their bullets would take a ripper down no problem. In the end, we'd decided to add an additional sniper to cover the other shooters, while they were doing their job.

Humans didn't draw rippers as quickly as magical creatures did, even though they didn't eat magical creatures. I think they sought us out of curiosity, or maybe we put something out there they could sense.

We hiked over to where the snipers would

take their stations, about a half mile away. It was the furthest from the target we could get that all the men still felt confident that they'd be able to make the shot. We'd flash a light facing them when it was time to take out the watches on the buildings. They took their places and we set off toward the plant.

With each step we took, the feeling that something was wrong grew in me. The plant was lit, but there wasn't any movement, not even on the towers. It was too silent. There should have been noise.

We all stood still, eyes only for the compound. A little flashing light caught my eye and I turned to see a lightning bug. It stopped glowing as it neared me and hovered by my ear. "All bad gone."

"What?" Cormac asked, standing close to me.

"Nothing," I said, knowing the bugs wouldn't speak to him.

The bug made a little buzzing noise and repeated in a high-pitched sound that was a strain to hear, "Gone."

"Does anyone hear that?" Cormac asked.

"Yeah," Dark said, "I do. I could've sworn I heard a baby's voice say 'gone.'"

"They're gone," I said in disbelief, not caring about explaining the lightning bugs to them.

"We don't know that yet," Crash said, sounding as equally dejected at the idea.

"She's right. They're gone. The rippers aren't there, either." Cormac stepped in front of us, staring at the compound.

"You can see where the rippers were?" Crash asked.

"I can see better, smell better and move faster than a regular human. I'm also a hell of a lot stronger. I've got a plethora of things I do better but I don't want to embarrass you by listing them all. Plus, it would take too much time."

Really Cormac? Was this the appropriate time for a pissing contest? I just shook my head and started forward.

Cormac followed me. "Where you going?"

"Down to see if they left anything behind."

He didn't say anything but he must have agreed because he followed me.

"Don't you people want to make sure they aren't there first?" Crash called after us.

"They aren't," I yelled back.

Dark and Colleen followed first and the rest of our people fell into step quickly after. Crash's men started to follow after we were halfway there. Close enough behind to make sure they didn't miss anything, but far enough back to let us take the brunt of an attack.

Cormac tilted his head upward as a breeze blew in. "This isn't going to be pretty," he said.

"What are you picking up?"

"Prepare yourself. The smell of death is pretty thick."

Sometimes having regular senses had benefits.

Cormac grabbed the bottom of a chain link

fence with barbed wire on top and stretched it upward, making an opening.

"Do you hear anything?"

"Nothing," Cormac said.

"Me either," Dark added. "Should we stay together or take the buildings like we planned?"

"I'm going to head over to where the rippers were, to make sure it's clear," I said.

"Why don't the rest of you take the buildings together, just to be safe. Colleen goes with you and I'll go with Jo."

Dark nodded. Having an even keener sense of smell than Cormac, he knew what was going on. Whatever it was, it was right where Cormac and I were heading.

It didn't take long after we left for the smell to hit me. I wondered how Cormac could breathe, with his stronger senses. I pulled my shirt up over my nose and mouth but it did little to help.

It didn't matter what I saw, I needed to keep it together. I didn't have the luxury of being able to fall apart. No one did, not anymore. In this world, if you fell apart you got ripped apart, eaten for breakfast. These times were only for the strong. Darwin would've had a ball if he were alive.

We walked into the area where I knew the rippers had gathered. They were gone but the remnants of their recent, and not so recent, meals were scattered throughout the courtyard.

Please don't let them be human parts, please. I took a step forward into the carnage and the first thing I noticed in the blood and gore was a baby's hand. The wrist was still there, but not much more.

All thoughts of being tough and a bad ass died right there. Tears streamed down my face as I dry heaved, grateful that nerves had kept me from eating too much today.

I felt Cormac's hand on my back and I stood up quickly, embarrassed.

"It's okay," he said as I stepped away. "It's a natural reaction."

"I don't see you throwing up." I wiped a sleeve across my face, not exactly an elegant gesture, but neither was the scene.

"No. But I've seen a lot of battlefields. I've got too many layers of scar tissue, built up over the years." He wasn't gloating; it was a matter of fact statement. "Trust me, you'll get there. Few hundred years and you won't be fazed either."

"Few hundred? Is that the current pace of desensitization?" I asked, making a joke because this was a laugh or cry moment.

"In good times, it takes a little longer, but peace never lasts long anywhere. When a country crumples, it's never a pretty situation," he said and walked around the courtyard, looking from body part to body part.

I stood, and tried to move around the area that was the size of a soccer field without stepping in blood. It was impossible, so I settled for not stepping on flesh or shredded clothes.

"How many do you think were killed here?"

"At a glance, it's impossible to say accurately, but at least a hundred."

I scanned the area, looking for something I'd recognize of Sabrina's, but dreaded finding it. I opened my mouth to say we needed to get Dark, but then I stopped. Dark, in wolf form, would be able to smell if a part of Sabrina was here, and I decided I'd rather not know. If she were dead, maybe it was better to be uncertain than find a piece of her mutilated flesh.

"So many limbs," Cormac said, in a cold scientific manner, while I was barely holding it together.

I took a deep breath before I told him my thought. "They like feeding on the torso and the brain, and they were fed plenty enough that they could be choosey." I gagged on the stench again.

"Some of these are fresh," Cormac said and I saw him actually touch a hand, sticking up from a pile they had made.

"What are you doing?" I asked. Sometimes the way Cormac could shut down his feelings scared me and this was a perfect example.

He looked over from his squatting position near the pile. "I'm trying to get a read on how long ago they left."

"Jo?" It was Colleen's voice in the distance.

"I'll be there in a second, Colleen. Wait there!" I frantically started to make my way toward her voice.

"Jo, what are you doing?" Cormac asked.

"I don't want her to see this. She's so young and she's seen so much. I can't let her see this too. I just can't."

I didn't know why but Cormac had a sad look in his eyes as I rushed as quickly as I could across the field. I had to shield Colleen from this.

But it was too late. There she was at one of the openings to the courtyard. I expected crying and screaming but her eyes just sort of glazed over.

"Are you okay?" I asked as I neared her.

"Yeah. Did you find her?" Colleen asked as I watched her start to move through the mutilated body parts and blood. "If you didn't, Dark can, I'm sure."

I walked closer to her and put a hand on her arm. "You don't have to act tough."

"I'm not. I've seen scenes like this before." She pulled away from me and went back to looking through the courtyard. "Not as many, maybe, but when it's your family it packs more of a punch. Most of the humans in the casino have seen stuff like this. What do you think was happening while you all were making your way back from New York?

"No one even saw it coming. There was no chance to hide or even fight. The humans aren't just pissed off about what happened to the world, they're pissed off at watching their loved ones get ripped apart in front of them."

It took a minute to find words again and even when I did, I could only think of one. "Sorry," I said.

She turned back to me and now I could see the

unshed tears she was holding back. She was tough, but not as tough as she wanted everyone to think.

"I know. I also know enough to realize it was the only option. Burrom told me the whole story. They'll get over it. They just need time." She turned back and started walking through again.

"What did you find inside the buildings?" Cormac asked.

"Nothing much, just a couple of used food cans and garbage. There was a room that looked like it might have been a holding cell, but we couldn't tell for sure," Colleen said.

"There was something strange about one of the rooms," Dark added as he walked into the courtyard.

"What?" I asked.

"Hard to describe. You should go look," Dark said. "I picked up Sabrina's scent in there."

"Dark, can you switch?" Cormac asked. What he didn't say was check and see if you catch her scent out here with the rest of the dead, but he didn't have to. We all knew what Cormac wanted.

"Sure," he said as he started to unbutton his shirt.

Dark explained where the strange room was and I was happy to leave the blood and gore behind. I didn't care what we found, it would be better than staying in the courtyard another second.

We headed toward the inner building that was dead center of the development. The door was wide open when we got there and the lock didn't look broken. When they had taken over this place, it must have been occupied and I wondered if some of the body parts lying in the courtyard now were among its original inhabitants.

We climbed to the second floor and headed down the hallway. There were only two doors and we took the one on the right, as Dark instructed.

It was already cracked a couple of inches and I nudged it open the rest of the way with the toe of my boot. It was a decent sized room, maybe twenty by twenty, with a tiled floor but its walls and ceiling were blotchy with black marks everywhere. It looked like it had been used as an office with a desk in the center and a couch off to the side.

"What is this? It looks like burn marks but why would they be shiny?" I said, as I got closer to one spot.

"Don't touch anything."

"Wasn't planning on it."

"Dark was right. Sabrina was in here. I can smell her scent strongly," Cormac said, circling around the room.

"Cormac? Jo?" Crash's voice sounded from the hallway and then he was at the door. He paused for just a moment to take in the scene and then continued. "Dark's picked up their trail."

When Crash turned and left, neither of us hesitated to follow. This might be our only chance of getting Sabrina back. If we let the trail grow cold again, we might never find her.

"I'll send two guys to get the Hummers and they can catch up with us after they get them," Crash said. "We're going to need the supplies they carry if this takes a while."

"Did they go on foot?" I asked as we ran down the stairs behind him, heading out to where the rest of the group was.

"Dark thinks so," Crash replied.

"Tell your guys not to give away our location when they catch up with us," Cormac said.

"I'll be in communication with them the whole time. They'll keep their distance. They're trained. These men were the elite of the military before this, give them a little respect."

"I give respect when it's earned. Not before."

Crash ignored Cormac and walked toward the group.

"Must you always prove that you've got the biggest dick in the room?" I asked Cormac under my breath as we walked after him.

"I wonder what made you choose that particular wording?" he asked in mock wonder.

Crash's three snipers were preparing to leave the group as we approached and Rogo stepped over.

"I need a word with you," he said to Cormac. I watched Cormac go off to the side with Rogo and nod his head at something he said. He headed back quickly leaving Rogo standing in the same spot.

"What's going on?" I asked Cormac but my

eyes still on Rogo who was pulling off his shirt. I turned back to Cormac when Rogo started undoing his pants.

"He's leaving."

"To where?"

"Back to the casino."

A loud roar filled the air and I saw Rogo in his wolf form. The guy was an ass but I couldn't deny his wolf form was superb. Seeing him like this made it clear why he was alpha. His wolf eyes looked directly at me and his lips curled back over massive fangs.

Then Cormac looked at him and took a single step in his direction. I couldn't see Cormac's face with his back to me, but I saw Rogo bow his head quickly, losing his aggressive stance and taking off in the direction of the casino.

Cormac turned back to me. "It's better that he's going," he said. "If this trail leads to the senator, I'm not sure he wouldn't end up fighting against us. I still want him alive right now."

I stored that information away for later. If Rogo did end up knowing something about my mother, I had resigned myself to killing him. Now I knew I wasn't going to get too much grief from Cormac if it happened.

The senator was a much larger problem. I was about to issue another word of warning to the group but then I really looked at them, maybe seeing them for the first time. Dark was in wolf form and didn't look like he was planning on shifting back, his clothes packed away. Colleen had her hands out in front of her, streaks of electricity bouncing back and forth between her fingers.

Crash looked almost as stone faced as Cormac did. I knew he'd do anything he had to do to get his kid back, including running a knife through me, if needed.

The two new additions also looked like they could hold their own. Evan was flexing his hands out, sharp claws extending and retracting back into his fingers as he did so. Sharon, who was stunning to the point it was hard not to look at her with her caramel colored skin and waist length black hair, was impossible to keep track of. Colleen had said she was like a ninja and that was probably an understatement. Sometimes you saw her and then she just disappeared. You'd look around and find her right back in the same place as before. It was slightly unsettling. Katie was hoping around, unfazed by the disaster. I swear the girl had to have a stash of antidepressants, somewhere. There was no point in warning her.

These people didn't need warnings, they had seen as much as me, maybe more. Who was I to lecture anyone on the risks?

CHAPTER TWENTY-FIVE

We followed their trail five miles north. The early dawn light was streaked across the sky when it became obvious that they had headed in a straight line to route fifteen. We gave up following on foot and piled into the Hummers that caught up to us quickly. Cormac, Evan and Dark, the three who could see the best, kept a vigilant eye on the road ahead, hoping to spot them before they saw us.

I never thought I'd be able to sleep, crammed in the back of a truck surrounded by people who should be my enemy, but I leaned against the door and was out.

When I awoke, my head and upper body were leaning against Cormac. The sun hung right above us and we were still on the road.

"Where are we?" I asked as I straightened up

and looked out the side window. When I turned forward, my breath caught in my throat. It was the tornado wall. It couldn't have been anything else. It looked like a wall of sand from where we were, reaching miles and miles high.

"We're about ten miles outside the border of the senator's territory," Cormac said by my side.

"It could be worse," I said in a voice loud enough that Crash's men could hear over the sound of the car. *Holy shit, we're completely fucked,* was a more accurate description of my inner monologue.

"They must have crossed into the senator's territory by now," Crash said.

I looked at Cormac, silently asking if we believed him, and he nodded in response.

Both trucks pulled over before we got much further, everyone knowing instinctively it was time to regroup. I stepped out of the truck, taking a swig of water and not the whiskey I craved. I'd need all my wits about me for this, and contrary to popular belief, I didn't *have* to drink.

Crash nodded his head over to the side and I followed him as he ducked behind the back of one of the trucks and out of sight. I stepped around the truck, knowing in my gut what was coming.

"I've got to leave."

"I figured." I let out a long breath.

"That cluster of buildings up there is a border town. Find a guy called Lizard Man. He can get you across."

"What are we going to find on the other side?"

"It's not much different to here, but the senator has spies everywhere." He leaned over and peeked around the truck. "I can't have the rest of the guys see me helping you again. Trust me, it's better for us to split now. Once we cross over, if you want any element of surprise then you don't want these guys with you. I think some of them might already be feeding information back to the senator."

A noise caught both of our attention and he started walking in the opposite direction. "Good luck," he mouthed to me, right before he moved out of sight.

I walked around the opposite corner of the truck and saw Cormac waiting there, not looking too happy.

"It was business."

"I know, I was listening."

"Do you not want to go? But then..." I didn't need to finish what I was thinking. Trap or not, we might not be able to find them if we didn't continue. "I think we have to."

"I agree."

We walked back over to where the group was forming. The few people that had moved out of sight for a moment, to handle needs, were filing back. Crash was already explaining to the group that he and his men were parting ways with us at the entrance of the border town.

They drove us the last short distance and

parted ways with barely a goodbye. We walked into the small town that was as much rubble as anything else and I was amazed at the tenacity of the human spirit. People walked here and there, and even in the midst of so much destruction, it still felt like a community.

They passed by us as we walked into their city, and except for a few skeptical, worried glances, they left us alone. When I heard the click clack of horse hooves approaching, I knew they were heading for us. This is why nobody bothered us. They had alerted some sort of vigilante police force that was keeping the peace.

A man and a woman, both on dark brown horses, turned the corner and came into view. They both cradled rifles in their arms but they weren't pointed at us, not yet anyway.

"What can we do for you folks?" the woman asked.

They weren't in uniform but they had yellow stars made of fabric sewn to their shirts. I relaxed after hearing her question and seeing their still at ease postures. These people weren't looking for trouble. They were trying to keep it out.

"We're looking for the Lizard Man," I said.

The couple didn't reply right away as they spoke to each other.

"Why?" the woman asked.

"Safe passage, that's all. We mean him no harm."

I wasn't sure why this seemed funny to the

two of them but they laughed for a couple of seconds and then gave us directions to where we could find him. They left with a quick warning not to disturb the peace.

Walking through the town streets was strange. The deeper we got in, the more activity there was. There even appeared to be a school, or maybe a daycare. A couple of adults watched about ten kids playing in a field with an intact swing set.

Further down at the next intersection, a few make shift tables were set up with vendors and people bartering for food. I pulled an energy bar from my pack as my stomach started growling at the smells. One table was laden down with vegetables and the other with breads. How were they doing so well here? There were no farms around, so I wondered where their food source was coming from. We didn't have fresh vegetables and we had more resources than it looked like they had. We all looked at each other in bafflement.

Every so often, a *changed* would walk by and I'd have to stop myself from gawking. It would be easier if they had all turned into something similar, but there didn't seem to be anything uniform about the mutations.

The one approaching us was covered in what looked like alligator skin and had yellow eyes; another flew overhead with fluffy white down wings, looking like a cherub. It was going to take me a long time to adjust to this.

"That's it," I said. It was a small yellow ranch

house on the outskirts of the main town. It was surprisingly intact, compared to the rest of the buildings. It made me wonder if Lizard Man was a VIP of the town, or just among the lucky who had always resided here and whose house managed to fare better.

We kept Dark to the back of the group, if not completely out of sight as he was still in werewolf form. Then it was left to Cormac and I to bicker over who knocked.

"No one is going to answer the door for you," I said to him.

"Why wouldn't they?"

"Because you've had your scary face plastered on for the last two days."

A couple grunts in agreement came from our group.

"Now, will you back off and let me do it?" I asked.

"You should. If he's one of the *changed*, he'll like her more," Colleen offered.

"What do you mean?" Cormac and I asked at the same time.

"Me and some of the others were talking about it a couple of days ago. There's just something about you we all feel drawn to."

I was a bit stunned by that admission and the door swung open to the Lizard Man before I could reply. There was no doubt who it was. He stood on two legs but his torso was freakishly elongated. His skin was a mottled yellow-black and he didn't greet us with words but with a forked tongue tasting the air.

"How cansss I help yousss?" he asked, his words blending into hissing noises at the end of some of the words.

His eyes roved over the group of us and I saw a different glint when they landed on me. Colleen was right; the *changed* were drawn to me. Cormac must have recognized it too, because he actually let me take the lead, instead of doing our normal arm wrestle for control.

I stepped a few inches nearer without getting too close. "Give me Sabrina's picture?" I asked Cormac.

He dug into his pack and handed me a now well-worn photo of her.

"Have you seen this woman?" I held it up to him.

"I seesss no one," he replied staring forward, refusing to look.

"She's in trouble. We don't mean her harm."

He looked down at the picture and then back to me. "My business isn't to tellsss people'sss secretsss. If I *did* seesss her, I notsss remembersss for certain."

It was as much of a yes as we were going to get. "We need to get across. You're supposed to be the man that can help us."

"What do youssss have to paysss?" He eyed up our few supplies suspiciously.

I did a mental inventory. I doubted water

canteens and proteins bars were going to cut it.

"What do you want?" Cormac asked when I sputtered and stalled.

"Gunsss." Lizard man pointed to Cormac's holster.

"We'll give you five when we return."

"No. Nowssss." He shook his head adamantly.

"No."

"Yousss might not makesss it back."

"You can have mine now, theirs on our return," Cormac countered.

"Whensss?"

"How long will it take to cross?"

"One hoursss."

"We'll meet back here at nightfall."

CHAPTER TWENTY-SIX

We settled down in an abandoned building that was on the very outskirts of the town, taking turns keeping watch. Even though this little town looked to be about the safest place we'd seen since the destruction, it was all relative. Safe wasn't what it used to be. Not having the imminent threat of being shot or ripped apart was great and all that, but if you were smart, you still slept with one eye open.

I was half in and out of sleep when Dark got up from his place by the window and jolted me fully into the here and now. He was still in wolf form, which burned more energy and needed more sleep. That he still hadn't felt comfortable switching back to his human shape said it all.

I tensely watched him, not able to hear what he could. Then he relaxed and gave me a nod.

Whatever he'd heard wasn't a threat. It took another minute before I heard the footsteps that alarmed him.

Cormac stepped into the room, food cradled in his arms. We were all starving by now. We'd packed for a quick raid, not a camp out.

He'd gotten bread and some sort of smoked meat, there was even cheese.

"How did you get all this food?" I asked.

"If we make it back, we aren't going to have a gun or bullet between the lot of us."

"Did you find out where they're getting all their supplies?"

"They're bartering with the people on the other side of the wall."

"What do they have to barter with?"

"They wouldn't say."

If you didn't have food, and money meant nothing, there weren't too many things left to trade. If I had mouths to feed, I'm not sure what I'd be capable of doing to see them eat. No one judged, anymore. You couldn't. If you went down that road, you wouldn't have too many people left you could talk to. People did what they had to and no one talked about it.

What really struck me was how did the people on the other side have things to give?

We split up the chow, each making a sort of makeshift sandwich. Back in the day, this would've been smothered in mayonnaise. Now? I was just happy I had water to chase it down with.

I slowed down eating after a couple of bites, looking at how thin Colleen was.

"Don't you dare," Cormac said as he sat beside me.

"But look at her," I said under my breath.

"There's been enough food at the casino," he said.

"If you get your ration, there is. It doesn't look like she's been getting hers."

"She's with Dodd and Dark now. We'll get her fattened up when we get back."

If we get back, I thought to myself.

"You try and give away your food right now and I swear I'll take you down before you even get to her."

"I got it. I'm eating."

I knew he was bluffing but I didn't feel like expending the energy to argue. I'm either becoming mature or I'm beyond exhausted. I covered the yawn that came with that thought. *Yeah, just tired.*

Cormac stood and grabbed his bag, pausing by Colleen and handing her the rest of his. She hesitated but he shoved it in her hand, forcing her with one of his scarier looks.

We packed up our few belongings, mostly just shirts used as makeshift pillows, and headed back over to Lizard Man's house. The town that had been bustling before was now deathly quiet and it showed how insecure everyone still was in their environment. Didn't matter if the rippers weren't here right now, you still knew they were out there, waiting. And maybe one night, if they got hungry enough, the tornado wall wouldn't keep them at bay any longer.

Our feet crunched along the ground as we walked down the streets. Flickering candle light allowed me glimpses of families trying to persevere in this harsh new world and occasional laughter proving they could.

Lizard Man was waiting outside of his house when we arrived.

"Gunsss?"

"One gun," Cormac said and reached for his holster to give him his.

Before he took it out, I laid a hand on his. "He can take mine," I said. I pulled it from the holster at my ankle that Cormac had insisted I wore. I'd hated the bulky nuisance from the second I'd put it on. I handed it to Lizard Man. "It wasn't much more than a prop anyway."

The Lizard Man tucked it into one of the zippered pouches on his pants and I wondered who had tailored them for his new form.

"Thisss waysss," he said.

I tried to act natural when he got on all fours with his shortened limbs and started to move like a lizard. I didn't think I pulled it off too well, so I was just grateful he was in front of us.

As we got closer to the tornado wall, I could make out the different individual cells within the massive dust they kicked up. I could see the lightning bolts striking the ground. The roar of the storms, which had been just background din before, was deafening.

Lizard Man held up a hand, signaling for us to wait. He moved along the sand, his tongue darting out continuously. Pausing for a minute, he appeared to be zooming in on one spot. Then he started burrowing into the sand at a rapid pace, sand being kicked behind him and piling up. An opening of about five feet by five feet emerged in the sand.

Looking at it, I already felt claustrophobic, even though I was standing in the middle of the wide-open desert. He stopped digging and waved us over before he disappeared into the tunnel.

Colleen grabbed my hand. Figured that she'd need support now. I was much better equipped to handle the gore in the courtyard but she was all miss independent then. I squeezed her hand with an assurance that I didn't feel.

Cormac stepped in first, almost bent at the waist, trying to accommodate his height. Dark dropped onto all fours and loped over with enough grace to make me realize he was quite versatile in this form. Katie, Evan and Sharon followed next. Colleen and I took the rear, with me ushering her in front so I could keep her going.

The noises subdued quickly as we entered and it was so dark I couldn't see Cormac in the distance, only black. Trying to keep my own abnormal breathing under control made me more aware of

Colleen's. I placed a hand on her shoulder and she gripped it tightly a second later.

"Use your lightning. It will help you see and make you feel better," I whispered to her.

"I don't want to look weak." She spoke so quietly that I didn't have the heart to tell her Cormac and Dark heard her anyway.

"Colleen," Cormac yelled from way ahead of us. "Can you light this place up a bit so the humans can move easier?"

The corners of my mouth tugged up. He'd never admit it but these people, the ones who lived in his casino, were becoming his people too. He could fight and deny it all day long, but I saw the signs.

"Be careful not to touch me when I do this," Colleen said. "I'm not sure if my whole body gets charged and I don't want to hurt you." Her voice already sounded better just from gaining some modicum of control over her situation.

I didn't see anything and I started to worry that she couldn't do it. And then she spread her fingers in front of her and it looked like she held a sparkler, except it was the tip of her finger.

"That's pretty," I remarked, never having seen that version. Normally, she would toss a ball of lightning back and forth in between both hands.

"Thanks. It's a new version I've been working on, but it's a bit harder to control." And would keep her mind more focused on something other than the dirt tunnel we walked through.

It was small but it gave off a lot of light and I could see at least another three miles of tunnel stretched out ahead of us. Now to distract *myself* from the feeling of being buried alive.

"Mr. Lizard?" I called ahead, not knowing what else to call him.

"It'sss Sam," he replied.

"Did you dig this out by yourself?" I asked, looking at the claw marks along the walls of the circular tunnel.

"Yesss, I like to dig now."

"Where does it let out?"

"Safe placesss. Turnsss left here."

I looked up to the left to realize there wasn't just one tunnel but an entire labyrinth. We twisted and turned as we went and the true genius of it became very clear. Even if you could find the entrance, you might never find your way out without him. The knowledge didn't do much to help my nerves.

He had said three miles and at about twelve minutes a mile...nope, too long. Don't think about that.

Deep yoga breaths, one foot after another, just keep going. On the plus side, the longer we were under, the less I cared about what was waiting for us.

It seemed like an eternity before the Lizard Man spoke again. "Staysss back, mustsss dig us outsss," he said finally.

It was amazing to watch him dig. He looked

just like a lizard would, or what they looked like on the nature channels. His arms worked in a flurry as the dirt kicked up and he burrowed through and then widened the hole.

"Shhhhh," he said as he waved his hand at us in a quick motion.

My hair was matted with dirt and I'd never felt grimier when we emerged from the hole. The tornado wall was far enough away to not feel like we'd be swooped off our feet at any moment but masked our sounds quite nicely.

Trying to get my bearings, I looked around quickly. A town sat in the distance, and I wondered if before the change, it might have been joined with the border town on the other side of the wall. Even though it was in rubble, there were dim lights. There were patches of plywood and tarps covering what I imagined were gaping holes in the roofs below.

From what I could see, there was only an occasional person or pair walking the streets, but they were out and about. That said more than anything else. They felt safe from the rippers at night here. Was that the senator's control, or were they just more confident of the tornado wall keeping them at bay?

"Samesss time tomorrowsss nite?" Sam asked.

"No, wait. We plan on returning tonight," Cormac instructed.

"Isss wait insss tunnel. Yousss stomp here whensss ready."

He moved to a spot about ten feet from the opening and stomped his foot on the sandy ground. It didn't make a sound from where we stood but you couldn't hear much over the storms.

We watched him bury himself back under the ground, disguising any opening had existed. Dark and Cormac scoured the area, trying to pick up a scent of them.

"Her scent is here but it disappears after a few feet," Cormac said.

"That's the most obvious place to start," I said and looking at the town in the distance.

"We'll go scout ahead," Cormac pointed between the two of us, "the rest of you stay here, out of sight. If we aren't back in the hour, you go back through the tunnel."

They agreed and we headed in to scope out the town.

Cormac and I stayed to the shadows whenever possible, working our way toward the closest house. Crouching by a nearby overgrown shrub, we peered into the window of a mostly intact colonial, built during the Mc Mansion explosion.

A woman and a man were sitting down at their dining room table with a girl toddler. It would have been the picture of domestic bliss if the man didn't have lobster claws for hands and the woman's skin wasn't an odd shade of green. The child was the only normal human in the room but odds were that she wasn't either. A regular young man walked in and placed plates down in front of the family and left the room, appearing to be a servant.

Cormac grabbed my arm, tugging me after him. We worked our way around to the side of the house that gave us a better view of what looked like the main drag of the town. Still hidden by shrubs, we watched as people walked about here and there, but the thing that caught my eye the most was a cluster of ten humans working in the center. Two men in fatigues stood nearby with whips in their hands as the men looked to be clearing debris out of a park. One of the men laboring stumbled to his knees under the weight of a large piece of concrete he was carrying. The larger of the two men in fatigues walked over and violently whipped him until he rose.

Every single one of the workers appeared to be a normal human.

What the hell was going on here? I turned to Cormac and gave him a look. He nodded in agreement, thinking the same thing I was. The *changed* here were making slaves of the regular humans. It didn't make sense, though. They were only ten percent of the population. Even with powers, they could be overwhelmed by the humans without too much trouble.

"I want to go see what's in that building over there," he said, pointing to what looked like it might be a town hall. The building was out in the open and was going to be hard to approach.

"You go," I said, knowing he had a better shot of checking it out on his own. "I'll wait here. You'll draw less attention alone."

My eyes went immediately back to the group working, once Cormac left, wondering if there was some way to help them before we left.

CHAPTER TWENTY-SEVEN

"Hello, Jo."

It was the senator's voice. I knew it by heart because I'd heard it over and over again every evening in my nightmares. I stood up from my kneeling position on the ground and dusted myself off leisurely before I turned around.

He stood about fifteen feet away and was as attractive as he had been last time, all blond and golden, dressed in a dark pin striped suit. He seemed more comfortable in his skin now, not that it had been that long since I last saw him.

About twenty military men stood around him, Crash among them. I briefly caught his gaze and saw the apology there, not that it mattered to me. My thoughts didn't linger on him long as I saw rippers slowly making their way over toward where we were. They were moving closer and closer, their numbers swelling as I watched.

"What can I do for you?" the senator asked, seeming supremely confident in his position.

I closed the distance between us by five feet and watched his face. He kept his fake grin in place but I could see him watch every step I took in his direction, annoyed I wasn't cowering. I wasn't going to let him think I was scared of him.

I stopped walking and picked the spot where I'd stand my ground. "My people are over here. I've come to collect them."

"Did you not like the terms Oslo delivered?" His eyebrows arched. The smugness of his delivery grated on my nerves like nails on a chalkboard.

The rippers were gathering behind him in a way that demonstrated he had quite a bit of control over them. If he told them to attack me, would I be able to stop it?

"I think we need to discuss terms that would be more agreeable to both of us." That sounded diplomatic. I could swing this. I didn't *have* to be a hot head.

The bastard smiled full force now, as if he'd taken my measure. I got the sense that because I didn't go on the offensive, he thought I was powerless.

"No, I'd rather not negotiate with the likes of you," he replied, confirming my impression. He lifted his hand; dark smoke sprang from his palm and started to twirl around. "Take her down."

I initially thought that he was going to send the smoke for me like he had the last time but that would've been stupid. I'd beaten him at that game before. Then the rippers took a step forward. The dark smoke could control them, just like mine.

There had to be over a hundred rippers gathered by now, who were all suddenly fixated on me alone. They started to hiss and click, the sounds I associated with their attacks. I didn't know if I'd be able to keep them all at bay or what range I'd have, so I waited for them to edge in closer. I knew my emotions were churning close to the surface and I hoped the magic wouldn't be an issue.

Four feet, three feet..."Stop!" I screamed, white smoke was pouring out of me so thickly I was surprised I didn't choke on it. Truth was, I wouldn't have even known it was there if I didn't see it floating in front of my face. The rippers instantly froze.

Do I press it and try to turn the rippers back on him? It could fail. I couldn't risk failing in front of him and showing him a weakness. I decided to try something easier that I was confident I could pull off.

"Back up a few feet, you're in my space." The rippers pressed back almost instantly, shoving at the ones behind them.

I kept my eyes trained on the senator so I could watch as he lost some of his cocky attitude. He looked more pissed, now. Good.

"Are you ready to negotiate?" I asked, feeling a

bit smug and not hiding it.

"Let's take a walk," he said, getting his composure back too quickly, as if he had expected that result, even if it did anger him.

He moved forward and the rippers kept their distance as he moved closer to me. He waved off his men as they took steps to follow him.

It was a good thing too, because I drew the line at walking with Crash. If you're my friend, great. If you're my enemy, that's fine too. I understood why he did it and I didn't hate him. But you're one or the other and he'd officially picked sides.

I didn't say a word and waited for the senator to speak as we walked alone. The person that feels like they have to fill the air somehow always seems weaker. It helped that I didn't have any desire to talk to him.

"You're proving to be a bit of an issue to me."

"I'm glad you hold me in such high esteem," I replied sarcastically.

"But you are human, like the rest of the Keepers, and have the typical frailties associated with that form," he continued on, in a manner that seemed to be more of an internal monologue than a conversation.

I looked around the town's street while I waited for his next revelation and the sound of a crowd jeering became noticeable. I couldn't see them yet but as the noise rose I knew that's where we were headed. The knot in my stomach told me I wasn't going to like what I saw when we turned the corner.

"You aren't without your own weaknesses," I said. It was an empty threat, driven by the fear knotting inside of me.

"I was then, but not so much now. Not in this environment."

"And what if the world were to change back?"

"That isn't a concern. There is no going back."

The roar got louder as we turned the corner. I stood on the top of the street and looked below to where it sloped into a valley and my heart started beating so hard I felt like it was going to burst from my chest. Cormac was in the center, bloodied but standing, surrounded by at least a hundred men in fatigues. He'd already killed twenty or so of them by the count of the men lying dead at his feet. Watching, I saw him rip apart another two just since we'd arrived.

"I don’t think you have enough men."

"They are just a stall tactic to keep him in one place for a bit. The snipers are the ones that are going to take him down."

"It's not going to be that easy with the way he's moving," I said, hoping Crash hadn't told him about what one of their bullets had done to my shoulder.

"I only need one good shot with the bullets I'm using. I believe you know about those?"

I wanted to tear him apart right then and I let it show on my face when I looked at him.

"If you were able to kill me, which I'm not so certain you can, my snipers will open up everything they have on him. Are you willing to bet his life?"

I looked down at a man that had once been my enemy and realized I'd give my life for him if that was what it took.

"Name your terms."

"I'll let you walk from here with all your people."

Huh?

"Except Sabrina."

And there it was, the shot to the heart. It wasn't my life I'd have to sacrifice for Cormac, it was Sabrina's. "Why?"

"The ones that hijacked the group were also humans you call the *changed*. The leader of this group has taken a liking to Sabrina and I have my reasons for wanting to keep him happy."

So many things weren't making sense. Why didn't he just kill me the same way he could kill Cormac right now? Why let us leave at all? It was like a jigsaw puzzle but I was missing half the pieces.

"I want to see Sabrina."

"That's not a problem. She's close by."

"And nothing happens to him while I do. Or all bets are off."

"This way," he said and we started walking down another block. I could see the people pulling back quickly from their windows as we did. They were terrified of him and they should be. As calm and logical as he was acting right now, I couldn't get past the feeling that he might go bonkers in a split second. He wasn't just evil, he felt unstable. Evil could be predicted. Crazy was a lot more dangerous.

"They're in there," he said as we stopped in front of a charming looking colonial, about a block away from where we'd left Cormac. "It's just a temporary situation, while we waited for you." He smiled. "I wouldn't want you to waste your time if you try to come back."

"I want to see her before I decide."

He shrugged and waived his hand. The door opened immediately, proving whoever was in there had been watching and waiting for our arrival.

Another man in fatigues stood by the open door.

"Have Sabrina brought out, as well as the others."

He went back into the house without a word. Less than a minute later, the familiar faces of the *changed* walked out the door. Of the initial ten requested, there were only eight here. Colleen was hopefully still hiding back by the tunnel, and we'd found one dead in the desert. I counted the heads as they came out.

More men in fatigues walked out with them and waited on the lawn. When the *changed* would've come closer, the men stepped in front of them, blocking their way.

Then Sabrina was there and I watched as she

took a step out the door. Sabrina was immediately followed by a creature a few feet taller than her and completely covered in blood-red scales. He stalked her movements and grabbed her arm when she moved more than a foot in front of him. Dread filled me. There was no way I was going to make this work. No way I'd ever be able to leave her here like this with that animal.

"Gulagh," the senator said, "alone."

The creature's eyes blazed and massive wings I hadn't initially noticed spread out behind his back spanning at least ten feet. He let out a blood-curdling screech and tipped his head back. A line of fire spewed from what once might have been a human mouth. This was what had caused the burn marks in the building.

Sabrina stepped away from him and I could see she was walking with a limp, probably a break that hadn't been taken care of and healed wrong. I saw the way her eyes darted toward the creature as if she was waiting for him to drag her back at any moment. This confident and beautiful woman had become a timid beaten down shell of herself, in such a short time. My heart was breaking. We were prepared to die fighting, but not for this.

I was surprised that the senator walked away when she finally reached me. He walked back to Gulagh, where he waited on the lawn.

Up close, I could see she had changed more than I realized. The same type of scales that had been on her stomach, now covered her entire forehead.

"Are you okay?" I asked, already seeing the answer written all over her.

She opened her mouth to speak but couldn't get the words out. When she looked away from me to hide the emotions roiling in her, I moved with her, grabbing her shoulders.

"I'll figure something out, just..."

She shook her head immediately. "Stop. I know what the offer is. They've told me everything. I need you to take these people and leave."

'These people' were the huddled mass of eight, standing on the lawn, and Cormac.

"I won't just walk away and leave you here." I couldn't, not now that I had seen her. Even if they didn't kill her physically, she wouldn't make it mentally.

"Look at me," she said. Then as if afraid to be overheard, she mouthed the words *you cannot win.* "Believe me, I know. And it doesn't matter. I'm becoming whatever he is. Look at my face."

"So what? You can't walk down the hall these days without seeing someone different."

"But how can I...this was my choice. You've got to. I can do this," Sabrina said. Tears were streaming down her face and I realized my own were as well.

"You didn't know. I can't leave you here."

"I won't come with you willingly. This is my choice." I couldn't say anything else, because she turned her back on me and walked away, back to the creature that stalked her every move. I watched her step into the house and not look back once.

And I knew that if I tried to take her, I would be killing those eight people staring at me now. Worse, I'd be killing Cormac. I'd dealt with more than I thought I'd ever be able to handle, but losing Cormac...I couldn't even think beyond that.

"Are you ready to choose, Jo?" the senator asked as he walked up next to me. "Or do you need a few more minutes?"

I looked at the people on the lawn who were staring at me as if I was their last lifeline, then to the house where I knew Sabrina was trapped with that horrible creature. And then there was Cormac. I put my head up and straightened my spine even though I felt as if I were being pulled to pieces.

Emotions I couldn't afford overwhelmed me and I walked a few feet away from him. I needed to get a handle on myself. If I wanted to save these people, I needed to be the girl that didn't care about anyone, that could get through anything. I needed to shed the softness I'd developed over the last several months.

I'm not sure how long I ended up standing there, coming to terms with what needed to be done, but I turned now and walked back to the senator.

I looked into his face and had to squash down the overwhelming hate in me. I couldn't afford that emotion, even if it was aimed at the most worthy of targets. Hate would open the door to feeling other things.

My face as blank and cold as Cormac's on his best day, I laid out my terms to the senator.

CHAPTER TWENTY-EIGHT

I left the senator standing in the road and walked over to the group on the lawn. "We're leaving. Can everyone here walk?" I tried to gauge their conditions. I was skeptical about their mobility, but they all nodded.

"Then come on." I turned back to the senator. "Tell your goons to stand down when I get to Cormac."

I started to walk away from the house where I was leaving Sabrina, but not for long. I glanced back to make sure the eight were following me. They were, even if it was in a bit of a ragtag fashion. One of them, who looked like he was still in his teens, appeared to be struggling, but two of the others had taken an arm each and kept him moving.

We made our way toward where the senator's

men had Cormac pinned down to the same location. There were several more dead bodies lying on the ground but plenty more waited in the wings as he took out one after another. He was covered in blood, but if it was his, it wasn't slowing him down. The snipers hadn't taken him out and that was all that mattered.

When we reached the top of the hill, I told my already bedraggled group to stay there. I didn't want them going near the senator's men surrounding Cormac. If I were them, and in their shape, I would've felt relieved. They looked more anxious.

"I'm coming back," I said to them. "We're leaving here."

As I started to walk down the slope toward them, all fighting ceased. The senator's men simply disengaged and moved out of Cormac's reach, and a path to him opened before me. He stood on the other side of the pathway, through the men in fatigues, but he didn't look relieved to see me. His stare moved upward, behind me.

I turned toward the top of the street, where Cormac was staring. On the other corner, opposite the eight *changed*, the senator stood, just watching. The senator's eyes met mine.

I broke eye contact first and slowly walked toward Cormac. He was alive and I was going to get him out of here. That's all that mattered.

When I finally stepped next to him, he looked down at me. "What did you do?"

"I made a deal with him. It's okay, trust me." It was a lie. It was far from okay, but I wouldn't get him out of here any other way.

"Don't lie to me," he said, not budging from his spot. "What kind of deal did you make?"

I'd known this wasn't going to be easy. But I *had* to get him to follow me.

"You shot me in the head. If I can trust you after that, then you need to trust me now." It was my ace in the hole. I knew the guilt he carried over that and if I had to turn it on him for his own sake, I would.

I took a few steps back toward the others, waiting at the top of the street. I turned to see if he would follow. I stood there and waited for him. It took him a minute but he finally did.

"This doesn't feel right," he said as he joined me, "but I'm trusting you."

I started walking again and I sensed him behind me. My ragtag group of survivors looked relieved to see us returning. The senator just watched our progression.

Once we made it to the group, I motioned them to follow us. Cormac walked by my side.

"Where's Sabrina?" Cormac asked.

"They're bringing her to the wall."

"Why? What did you agree to, that we are just walking out of here? I don't like this," he said grabbing my arm and halting our progress.

"I need you to trust that I have this worked out." He looked at me and I saw the struggle going on. He was agitated and he knew something was wrong. I knew I had only the tiniest control of the situation.

"Please."

I started walking and he relented again. I think it must have taken everything he had to do it. Continuing with a situation he didn't like was the exact opposite of what Cormac would usually do and I knew he was doing it for me.

It made my heart swell at the same time it was being crushed.

I picked up the pace a bit, hoping to get everyone to the crossing as quickly as I could. It was a strain on the group, but I felt the time bomb that was Cormac ticking loudly.

"It's okay," I yelled out as we approached the place where we had left Dark, Colleen and the rest of them by the tunnel.

They stepped out of their hiding places slowly, and I knew that the senator and his men weren't too far behind us.

I stopped once I reached them and turned to see the senator, about fifteen feet back. He'd been following us the whole way, but I'd expected that.

Cormac looked around at the group and the senator. "I don't know what you did, but I'm not leaving here without Sabrina," he said to me, never losing eye contact with the senator. He thought that was the bargain I wasn't telling him about. That Sabrina was staying and that was fine. I just needed to get him past the wall before he knew the real deal.

A distant howling noise filled the air as small group of men appeared around the corner of a building in the distance. In the center of their group, I saw Sabrina. The howling must have been Gulagh.

We watched as they got closer, until they stopped by the front of the group where the senator stood. And this was as far as I'd worked the plan out.

"What is going on?" Cormac asked again. "If they are letting her go, why are they letting us leave?"

"I'll tell you as soon as we get on the other side of the wall." I was so close. "It's only a few more minutes. I don't want to discuss it here."

He turned his head and the tension was near to bursting from him. He was looking for a fight that he knew should be there, but couldn't find it.

"The second we cross, not a minute later," he answered.

We watched as Sabrina walked forward, followed by the senator. Everyone else remained behind, as I knew they would.

Sabrina walked the last ten feet by herself and was welcomed back into our group.

The senator stood back but not idly. I could see him focusing on the wall and an opening appeared through the storms. I just had to get them on the other side.

"Why?" Cormac barked out toward the

senator. "You're just going to let us go? What are you getting?"

"Jo has promised to never cross this barrier again," the senator said.

"And that's it?"

"That's all I wanted," he finished.

It was the truth.

"Let's go," I said, tugging at Cormac. He knew something was wrong but he took my hand and went with me anyway.

"The very second," he said.

Dark crossed first and then the humans. Cormac and I were the last to enter the opening. True to the senator's word, nothing happened until after the last vulnerable human had made their way out and it was only Cormac and I left in the opening.

I didn't know how long I'd have so as Colleen took her last step out of the opening, I turned to him.

"I'm sorry," I said to him quickly.

"What did you do?"

His eyes narrowed before he grabbed my hand, eyed up the distance to the opening, and started to run, pulling me with him.

"I did it for you," I tried to scream, but the noise of the storms were getting louder and closer and I didn't think he heard. And then his hand was gone as he was torn from me. "Cormac!" I screamed as the winds kicked up another notch and propelled him to the other side.

I couldn't see anything but sand as a strong wind pushed me back in the direction of the senator. Even as the winds kept my momentum going I still didn't turn, but kept my eyes on the wall of sand, hoping to catch a glimpse of him, just one last time.

Then I heard my name. It was barely there over the roar and I couldn't even imagine how Cormac had managed to shout that loud but he was alive and okay.

I turned to face my fate.

The senator stood there, waiting for me, with his men behind him and the rippers not far in the distance.

"You promised, even if he comes back, he won't be touched. None of them will be," I said as I paused before I closed the last distance.

"Yes," he said.

I heard the truth again in his words. He would honor the deal we had made.

I dropped my head, feeling defeated but resigned. They would make it. Cormac would be okay. He would understand why I did it. I took a few more steps forward.

When I got within a couple of feet from him, he waved one of his men forward. "You'll understand if I need to take some precautions."

I could have easily taken on the man who approached with the handcuffs but I'd made the deal. There was no turning back.

The senator looked on as his man finished

handcuffing me. "Don't forget the tape."

As I watched the piece of duct tape cover my mouth, I knew why it was done. Without being able to speak and with my hands cuffed behind my back, I was seriously handicapped.

A man in a white lab coat stepped out of the crowd and approached me, a syringe in his hand.

"It's just something to sedate you. Make the whole process go smoother," the senator explained.

He had sworn I wouldn't be tortured. He said he had no intention of killing me. It didn't matter, because just living with him like this was going to be torture but it was the price I'd been willing to pay. I'd bide my time until I knew I was stronger, then I would kill him; but my plans had rested on being cognizant. If I was doped up all the time, there was no hope.

I felt the cuffs on my wrists but there was nothing I could do. I couldn't speak. I needed my hands, at the very least. Panic shot through me at the years that rolled ahead in my mind. I didn't know if I'd ever die of natural causes; I could spend an eternity like this.

The man in the white coat was next to me, holding the syringe up, removing any air bubbles, when the ground started to shake violently. I fell to my knees as everyone scattered. They all sought cover and squatted down to avoid falling as the vibrations ripped across the ground. Even the senator ran as the earth shook more than it had since the shattering, when the greatest transformation had taken place.

It felt like the shaking was intensifying and was aimed right for where I was. I sat there, alone for twenty feet in every direction. A familiar buzzing whipped around my head and it took me a minute to realize it was the lightning bugs. "Jo, Jo," they repeated excitedly as the whizzed around me. "He's coming!"

I tried to ask who, but my voice was muffled by the tape.

"What, Jo?" one of them asked. "We can't hear you, Jo!" another chimed in.

"Wait! Maybe without the tape we can hear her!"

A chorus of "ahhh" followed. They converged on my face and I felt the tape being pried from my skin.

"Owww, I'm stuck! I'm stuck! I'm gonna die!" I heard a little voice scream out.

"You're fine, Lucy!" came another voice. "There."

"Don't yell at me! You didn't get stuck to that yellow paper for a day! I have PTPS!" Lucy yelled back.

"You don't have Post Traumatic Paper Syndrome! Now help us."

I felt the tugging at my mouth again and the tape fell. I took a deep breath. "Who's coming?"

"Him!" they screamed in chorus. Now that I didn't have to keep my head still for them, I swiveled around and saw a hill in the ground that was growing before my eyes. It had everyone's attention, which was why no one was paying attention to the fact that a bunch of bugs were trying to save me.

The hill was about seven feet, when all of a sudden everything stopped shaking. The sand slowly started to slide down its sides revealing black hair. Another inch and it looked like there might be tan skin under all that sand clinging to what was starting to look like a human form.

The sand continued to slide down what I now could confirm was a man's form. When the sand was down to only a few feet high, the man stepped out of the pile and everyone there instinctively moved back a few more feet.

His whole body vibrated and the sand flew from his skin. Dark black hair, tanned skin, pale blue eyes, and muscled perfection stood there in the nude. The guy could have been Cormac's brother.

"Excuse the lack of apparel," he said as he took a few steps out of the small mound of sand still at his feet. "My traveling conditions aren't conducive to clothing."

I was on the fringe of screaming and trying to get to my feet to run for cover when the man, or whatever he was, walked over to me. Something about him made me hold my tongue and stay in place. It was the way he cocked his head to the side and the gait of his walk. I didn't know him but my gut told me I did.

"Time to get this mess worked out," he said. His hand reached down to help me up but I pulled back. "What's wrong, Jo? Don't you trust me?"

My jaw dropped and there was no way to hide the shock I was feeling. It couldn't be. No way. He was supposed to be underground for fifty years.

"Burrom?"

The corners of his mouth lifted and his eyes squinted slightly. The package was perfection and looked nothing like the stout ground Fae I'd helped send off to hibernation. But it was him. Somehow, underneath all those good looks, I could see him. Staring as I did now, I even thought I noticed a slight green tint in his black hair.

Who he was remained a mystery to everyone else there, but his alliance was clear to all as I let him help me to my feet.

"How did you know what was happening?" I asked.

The bugs came swooping around again. "We told him, Jo! We saved you, Jo!"

"Time to get this show going and get the hell out of here," Burrom said. "I don't like this side of the wall."

My heart sunk at his words. "I appreciate you coming, but it doesn't change anything."

"He'll let you leave."

"I made a deal."

"He'll reconsider. Just watch and see." Burrom cleared his throat and spoke loud and clear to the senator, loud enough that everyone could hear. "We'll be leaving now."

"The deal is done." The senator took a step forward, making, his determination clear. "She stays."

"I don't think so," Burrom said, not flinching and speaking a bit softer as the senator came closer.

"I don't know who you are, but I told you, the deal is done. Go back to your side and be glad I let you live."

Burrom closed the distance to the senator and I followed. I wasn't going to let him go down alone for me.

We got within a foot of him and Burrom dropped his voice even lower for his next words. "I know. And if you don't let us leave now, everyone here will know as well."

What the hell was Burrom talking about? I could see the senator blanch. Whatever he was saying had the senator on the ropes.

Burrom took a step closer to me and rested his hand upon the back of my neck in a menacing manner before he spoke again. "You might not know me, but I've been here a lot longer than you. I'm not willing to hand everything over that easy."

"You could lose as well. Are you willing to chance that?"

"What do you think?" Burrom asked, only having eyes for the senator.

I didn't know what was going on, but I was

getting the feeling I shouldn't be trusting Burrom, either. He pulled me in front of him and placed his other hand on my neck. *What the fuck?*

The senator didn't move, and neither did Burrom.

The senator broke the tension first. "I don't want to see any of you on my land again or I will take the chance." The senator turned his back on us and walked away.

"You were willing to kill me?" I asked Burrom, as we stood in the center together.

"Not here," he said, not answering the question or giving me the opportunity to know if he really would've or not.

Rage boiled up in me at this latest possible betrayal and the day's events. The fear I'd wanted to feel but couldn't. Or maybe, it was because I knew I was going to be able to leave this place and I didn't even know if Cormac would speak to me again. The feelings I'd been holding back rushed to the surface.

White smoke poured out of every pore in my body, the sky opened up above me as bolts of lightning flashed and claps of thunder filled the air.

Burrom looked startled as he took a step back. "Jo, calm down."

My hands shook in front of me and the bugs were whizzing past my head in a complete frenzy screaming, "Oh no! Jo's real mad, now," over and over again.

"Jo!" Burrom yelled. "You need to calm down."

The wind had started to whip around us and it hit me: whatever was going on right now, I was creating it and it was getting pretty scary. I looked at everyone staring at me, the horrified expressions on their faces was a jolt. Enough to start cutting through the well of emotion I was drowning in.

The thunder and lightning lessened as the smoke started to subside.

The senator had stopped and was looking at me. And when our eyes met this time, he was scared.

"You should be," I said softly as I watched him. I knew he heard me.

"Jo," Burrom said. "Not now."

"Why?" I asked, turning on him, forcing an answer.

"Because if you don't win, I'm not sure anyone will survive."

Burrom's words sunk in as well as his actions. I looked over to where the senator had rejoined his men and the many rippers, that looked less calm than they had an hour ago but still swarmed around him in a protective manner.

White smoke was still pouring out of my pores as I eyed up the scene. "Get him," I said, directing my words at the rippers.

The rippers instantly turned on the senator and chaos ensued as he had to quickly conjure up his own smoke to back them off and get them under control again, but not before they had torn through a few of his men, trying to reach him to rip him apart.

I turned to Burrom. "Now we can go."

CHAPTER TWENTY-NINE

Burrom burrowed through the ground and got us back to the other side. Lizard Man had disappeared into the ground and refused to come out while Cormac had repeatedly tried to force his way through the tornado wall.

All eyes were on us as we stood there. Cormac looked nowhere but at me and stood frozen for a second. Then he was on top of me, almost strangling me in his embrace. He didn't let me out of his sight the entire way back, but he also wasn't speaking to me. Cormac's only words were he was getting me back to the penthouse and not letting me out again. I didn't care. I was just grateful to be leaving there with him.

After Cormac let me go he looked Burrom up and down, shook his head and made a disgusted grunt. The way Cormac reacted to him made me positive he somehow knew who it was.

"Hey, don't give me grief for this," Burrom said. "I never would've picked a get up this pretty."

That was the end of the conversation. No one felt comfortable talking this close to the senator's lands, or anywhere, now that we knew even the bugs could have ears.

"Wow," was the only word I could think of when we got back to the Lacard a day later, and it was echoed by the rest of the group. It looked more like a castle than a casino. It was hard to find even a glimpse of the modern structure that used to be there, except perhaps for its size. I doubted castles this big had ever existed.

Our makeshift bridge had turned into a full-blown drawbridge as we crossed over the moat. I paused before we entered through the wooden doors that were once glass, to touch the stone of the outside wall. Yep, real stone. If this was a magical façade, it was a damn good one.

Dodd and Buzz were in the foyer, which should probably be renamed the great hall. It came complete with the biggest fireplace I'd ever seen. Inside, with remnants of modern furnishings still, wasn't as bad as the exterior. The magic had seen fit to spare our electricity, as well.

Dodd rushed toward Sabrina, only acknowledging the rest us with a glance and a nod as he embraced her. I watched her hand self-consciously move to her forehead where the scales had grown. I'm sure Dodd noticed them but it didn't look like he cared.

All pretense of acting as if he wasn't hopelessly in love with her was gone. He scooped her up in his arms despite her protests, and whisked her away from the hall.

"Where are the senator's men that were left behind?" Cormac asked Buzz.

"They tried to sneak out of here but we caught them and threw them into the dungeons."

"Dungeons?" I asked.

Kever came to stand next to Buzz. "Yeah, we've got dungeons now and it's the real deal." Then they both caught sight of Burrom. "Boss, you've got a brother?"

"No, and don't call him that again," Cormac said. "Penthouse in one hour. Only us. Kever, you watch the floor." As soon as Buzz and Kever left, I watched Cormac take off down the hall.

Burrom came over and stood next to me as I watched Cormac walk off. Shirtless and in his borrowed pants, he was getting quite a bit of attention.

"Still not talking to you?" he asked.

"Nope."

"He will."

"I hope."

"This is going to be good," he said, laughing at a joke I didn't get.

I saw Cormac stop in his tracks and look backward, as if expecting to see someone. Then he stormed back to me.

"Yeah, see you in an hour," I said to Burrom as

he grabbed my arm and pulled me with him. I wasn't sure what the situation was with us. It was hard to know exactly where you stood with someone who wasn't speaking to you.

He didn't let go until we walked into the bedroom and he shut the door. He still wasn't speaking as he started taking off his own dusty clothes.

"What's the deal? Are you kicking me out?" I asked, intent on getting some sort of acknowledgment out of him.

"No," he said. He finished undressing and threw his dirty clothes into a pile in the corner.

"You're just not talking to me?" I asked as I followed him around the room with my eyes.

"It's too hard right now."

"Why?"

He swung around to face me and I tried to ignore the fact that he was completely naked, but it was difficult. That whole bucket list and hot sex thing did enter my mind.

"Because I'm too..." he paused, shook his head and turned away for a minute. "You made a choice with me the other night and then you act as if it's only you again, the one woman show."

"I did it for you. He had snipers aimed at you."

"And if you had told me, you would've known I didn't need you to save me." He walked over to where his holster was lying on the night table, pulled out the gun, turned it on himself and shot it all within a minute. The bullet didn't even break the skin, just dropped to the floor.

I suspected he'd been experiencing some differences since the shattering and now I knew for sure.

"The senator has stronger bullets. You don't know how you would've handled those."

He didn't answer, just walked into the bathroom and started running the shower. I picked up the bullet from the ground and looked at it. I recognized the odd hue it possessed and realized it was one of the senator's.

I stepped into the bathroom, expecting to find him in the shower already. He was just standing there, arm outstretched, palm resting on the wall. His head was bowed and I could tell he was struggling with the situation. I got it. He was pissed about how things went down, but I'd done what I thought was best at the time.

"Should I leave?" I asked, not knowing what else to do.

I instantly knew those were the wrong words when his eyes bored into me. He didn't say anything, just walked over and pulled my shirt off.

He tugged off my pants but this didn't require and explanation. I still wasn't sure where we stood but I needed this more than him and the desperate way he was running his hands over my body made me think he might need it as much as I did.

His hands lifted me and my legs wrapped around his waist. He stepped under the hot water, pressed me up against the shower wall and impaled me on his erection in one deep thrust, covering my moan with his mouth.

He was almost violent in his need as he thrust into me fast and hard. I clung to him, pulled to his intensity. With each stroke, I could feel myself getting closer, his need driving my own. I looked into his eyes and lost myself. I heard him find his own release as I sagged against him.

"Did I hurt you?" he asked as he pulled back just enough to look at me.

"No." I ran my hands over his shoulders and pulled him back closer to me.

"I thought you were gone." His voice was ragged and I could feel the tension still in him. "I was scared and I don't get scared. I don't even know what to do with that emotion." He pressed even more closely to me.

"I did it for you. I couldn't let you die." I buried my face in his neck.

"I would've preferred death."

#

A little less than an hour later, my limbs turned to mush, I was waiting in the living room for everyone. Burrom showed up in ripped jeans and a snug shirt that clung to him, looking like he planned to make the most of his new form. Buzz strolled in next with Dark. Dodd came in a few minutes later, with Sabrina. That was it; no one else had been invited to this meeting, at Burrom's request. He said what he wanted to discuss had to remain between just us.

We all took a seat on the couches, except for Cormac. I was glad that other than losing some of the windows to stone, the penthouse had pretty much remained the same.

"Sabrina, are you okay?" Cormac asked.

Dodd's arm was around her shoulders, lending her emotional support. She looked so much more fragile than I'd ever seen her. I didn't know what she had gone through while she was with them, but it had done a real job on her. I wondered if she'd ever be the same.

She didn't look like she was okay at all, but she nodded her head. "When we were hijacked in the desert, they just stumbled onto us by accident. When they saw we were changed, they brought us back with them. Except for Jimmy, the guy with the horns. He had tried to fight and they made an example of him."

"How did you end up with the senator?" I asked.

"I explained to them where we were heading, hoping they'd see the larger picture. They did, it just didn't work out the way I'd hoped. They went to the senator and struck a deal."

"Care to fill us in now, Burrom, on why he let us leave?" I asked.

"Not everyone here knows this, and I don't want it talked about outside of this meeting, but I'm a Ground Fae. I enlisted the help of Jo to seal my sleeping grounds. That's when things started getting strange. Instead of sleeping for fifty years, which is typical, give or take a year or two, I slept for less than a week. And I think it's because of you," Burrom said, looking straight at me. "When you sealed me, what happened?"

I explained the steps I went through and the blast at the end. I told them how I hadn't thought much of it, not knowing what was normal.

"I'm going to speak freely now," he said, looking at me. I nodded. I trusted everyone in this room.

"When the senator helped your mother conceive, he used magic, the same magic that rules this world, to help her. I think you are linked to this magic, in a way that is much deeper than what would be considered the norm, even in these strange times."

"I don't get it. What are you trying to say?" Dodd asked.

"I think it's similar to a person's circulatory system and she's a main artery. I think the magic of this world flows freely through her, like a conduit. I think he's realized the same thing and is afraid to kill her."

"Why do you think this?" I asked.

"Because when you sealed the ground for me, you put more juice into it than one being could possibly possess. I've felt your magic and you've got a lot, but not as much as you can direct. You're like a lightning rod."

"And that's why the *changed* are drawn to me." I looked across the expanse at Sabrina, who was a perfect example. We'd gotten so much closer since the shattering, but I'd just thought it was the situation. It had happened with all of them.

"What if I die?"

"Who knows, but I'd rather not find out," Burrom said.

I wanted to ask whether he had really been willing to kill me, but I didn't want to tell the whole room that part. When we had rejoined the group, without a prior word about it, both Burrom and I had selectively chosen to leave that part out.

"But why do you look so much like Cormac?" Dark asked Burrom.

"I don't know, but I'm pretty sure that's on Jo, too." He pulled a cigar, rather than his pipe, out of his pocket and lit it. "Goes better with the new look," he explained to everyone in the room.

I leaned my head back on the couch. "This isn't going to be the end of it. The senator isn't going to leave us in peace," I said.

"No, he's not," Cormac agreed. "And we aren't going to wait."

My phone started buzzing at the same time as Cormac's. Then Dodd's chimed in, followed by Dark's.

We all scrambled to answer them, knowing there must be a problem when Kever burst into the room.

He paused inside the door, panting heavily.

"The portal," he got out in between ragged breathes.

"What?" we all screamed.

"It just popped open. They're coming."

"Who?" Cormac asked.

"The Fae and the wolves, all of them! Thousands of them!"

If you would like to know more about the author you can find her at www.DonnaAugustine.com or twitter at DonnaAugustine@Donnaugustine.com.

www.ingramcontent.com/pod-product-compliance
Lightning Source LLC
Chambersburg PA
CBHW051408170626
46809CB00006B/2065